Searching for Maya

A novel

Heather Rath

Manor House

Library and Archives Canada
Cataloguing in Publication

Title: Searching for Maya : a novel / Heather Rath.
Names: Rath, Heather, author.
Identifiers: Canadiana 2024047970X | ISBN
9781998938162 (hardcover) |
ISBN 9781998938155 (softcover)
Subjects: LCGFT: Novels.
Classification: LCC PS8635.A82 S43 2024 | DDC
C813/.6—dc23

Cover Art: Woman and red smoke: MG/ Shutterstock
Cover design and interior layout: Michael Davie
Published in 2024 by Manor House Publishing Inc.
452 Cottingham Crescent, Ancaster, ON, L9G 3V6
905-648-4797 – All Rights Reserved.

Description:
A young girl is raped by her priest and gives birth to a
daughter, Maya, whom she puts up for adoption to get a
chance at a better life. But Maya's mother cannot heal
the baby hole in her heart. When she finally escapes an
abusive relationship after 20 years, she searches for
Maya. Both mother and daughter, unknown to each
other, find themselves in the Maya country of Mexico,
and are followed by a stalker. Will they ever reconnect?

Funded by the Government of Canada 

For Norm, a Yucatecan at heart

Acknowledgements:

First, my thanks to you the reader - this book wouldn't be possible without you.

Sincere thanks to Mike Davie of Manor House who believed in my talent and took the time to guide me through the process.

A grateful thank you to:

My writing tribe near and far, especially the Bluewater Writers: Bob Boulton, Delia Petrucci-DeSantis, Mary Frost, Phyllis Humby, Bob McCarthy, Karen McIlwaine, Rhonda Melanson, Kathy Milliken, Lynn Tait, Najah Shuqair.

My original WIT (Writers in Transition) mentors: Debbie Okun Hill, Josephine Ryan, Peggy Fletcher, John Drage, Hope Morritt, Carmen Ziolkowski, Anne Beachey, Norma West Linder.

My former colleagues/writers/friends: Marlyn Horsdal, Peter Snow, Ritchie With.

A special thank you to authors Jeanne Ainslie for her insight and support; and to Mike Davie and Marcus Starr for their support.

- Heather Rath

Reviews:

Searching for Maya is the story of Mary Jane (MJ), a vulnerable 16-year-old, who is raped and impregnated by her parish priest. She is abandoned by her mother and forced to bear her unwanted daughter who is given up for adoption. Rescued and protected by a controlling abuser for many years, MJ finally develops the courage to escape and search for her daughter, Maya, who MJ believes is living in the Yucatan Peninsula, the central location of the Maya culture. *Heather Rath*, an award-winning author of short stories and travel writing develops in *Searching for Maya,* an exciting, suspenseful detective story. Sex, passion and desire co-exist with disgust, fear and hate. *Searching for Maya* is a page turner that shines with strong dialogue, interaction and scene description and is a pleasure to read.
- **Jeanne Ainslie,** author, *A Country Girl, Caribbean Moon* and *Stranger at Herring Cove.*

Rath captivates the reader with quick, clever and cunning suspense, clever plot twists, and delicious irony. A master of the craft.
- **Marcus Starr** – author, *Nora's Curse* and *Monsters in the Moonlight.* Two-time Odd And Cryptic Cup winner.

MJ escapes a controlling abuser and embarks on a search for Maya, the daughter she gave up for adoption after being raped in her teens. Her search is filled with danger as her abuser hunts after her with murder on his mind – Rath has created a suspenseful, gripping thriller that delves deeply into the hunted-haunted psyche.
- **Michael B. Davie**, author, *The Late Man*

Chapter One

1955

She remembers the assault as if it was yesterday. Not 24 years ago. When she was 16.

Father Martin Garcia looked beatific, as if newly returned from a visit to the Holy Shrine. His tousled coal-black hair curled around his head like a choir boy. His dark brown eyes shone like holy lanterns. His smooth skin reminded her of milk chocolate.

But his breath stank of alcohol.

MJ had mixed emotions about seeing this man in the white collar for atonement. Her mother was blind to the Father's roving eye and appetite for ripe girls.

Unfortunately, pieces of hay and corn tassel had clung to her underwear from her exploratory romp in the fields with classmate Alex. This organic material, discovered by her horrified mother as she sorted clothes for the weekly wash, had led to maternal lectures, threats, screams. These, in turn, had led to catechism instruction/prayers of forgiveness from the good Father Garcia.

Today was her third redemptive meeting with him. Feeling more and more uneasy with each one hour 'lesson' on Wednesday afternoons after school, MJ approached his office at the side of the grey-stoned Church with trepidation. She was not comfortable.

After another preamble of the Lord's forgiveness that barely registered with her, Father Garcia changed direction.

"My dear child," he crooned. "I am so happy to see you again. I think you realize now your poor mother's concern and I believe this should be our last meeting. You are, indeed, a lost lamb newly found."

His soft voice muttering these platitudes jolted her mind after all his penance talk. She stiffened with suspicion.

Then she froze before him, unable to fathom what was about to happen. Conscious of how he placed warm hands on her shoulders, she realized he was slowly turning her around so her back faced him. He approached from behind, pulling up, removing his black cassock. She heard the rustle of his garments.

"Brace yourself on the table," he softly ordered. "Lean over, please, my dear."

Her heart pounded. Her loins moistened. Her gut tried to warn her. Fear of the unknown, yet familiar, territory enveloped her.

Meekly, she did as he commanded. Her heartbeat quickened.

Softly, gently, he pulled up her skirt. She gasped. Surprised, shaken by her sudden moistness down there.

Slowly, from behind, he released her soft breasts from her bra beneath her t-shirt. Rubbed, stroked them softly until her nipples hardened. He knew how to stimulate her.

The pit of her stomach cried for more.

But her head pleaded STOP!

She held her breath. Felt his hardness press into her back. Her mind went numb. But her juices flowed.

He drew her closer. Huge hands covered, smothered her loose breasts. They roved slowly down, in circular motion, between her legs. Pulled down her panties. To her ankles.

She gasped.

"Open your legs," he breathed. She obeyed. Not knowing why.

And then he was inside her. Thrusting. Gasping. Huge. She cried out in pain.

And then? He came! The good Father moaned, groaned, pulled her body closer. Sticky liquid smeared her vagina and her thighs. It all happened so quickly she could not breathe. She hurt. Terribly. And yet…

She could not deny her own initial stimulation. Coupled with horror.

Quietly, he murmured in her ear. "My dear Mary Jane. This never happened. Remember that. You are absolved of all sin."

Confused, frightened, she began to weep.

"Nothing to cry about my dear. You have been redeemed. Pull up your panties like a good girl. Wash yourself well when you get home. You needn't return for any more sessions."

MJ remembers running into the Church basement washroom next to the room where she taught Sunday School, and vomiting. She remembers running home, feeling dirty and guilty, throwing open the unlocked front door screen, and panicking.

She remembers getting out the scrub pail, filling it with soap and water, grabbing the scrub brush and scrubbing the large kitchen linoleum floor for as long and as hard as she could. As if scrubbing the floor would wash away his filth inside her.

Her mother, constantly housecleaning to keep up the old rented house in Brighton, came upon her daughter on hands and knees, scouring the floor violently.

"What are you doing for goodness' sake, MJ?"

"Helping you clean," said MJ without stopping.

Later, in her room, she lay trembling on top of her bed.

How different, she thought, was this violent act of fucking and taking. She closed her eyes and relived her petting innocence with Alex. If only to remind herself that she had no original sin.

In the beginning, MJ's boyfriend, Alexander Davis in her 6th grade class, had introduced her to the thrill of sex. They had crawled through local cornfields together and one thing led to another.

"MJ, stop here. We're in far enough." Alex grabbed her by the ankle. She turned to look at him and then at the tall stalks surrounding them. "I'll make us a little nest," he said as he patted down the high thick corn stalks. Taking off his sweater, he gallantly laid it on the greenery.

"Can I touch you?" he asked.

She trembled with desire. "Yes."

Slowly, awkwardly, he touched her white blouse. Unbuttoned it. When he reached inside to feel her sweating breast, she shivered in anticipation. His lips met hers.

Groping clumsily, MJ felt the bulge between his legs. It grew as her hand lingered there.

MJ remembered how time had stood still. Somewhere in the distance she heard the drone of an engine from a plane and then the bark of a dog. But mostly, as she lay hidden by cornstalks with her hands roving over Alex's body and his over hers, she felt ecstasy.

In MJ's smalltown naivety, she had sinned with Alex. Looking back, much later, through the eyes of experience, all they really did was get hot and bothered. When her mother discovered strands of straw caught in her underwear, she began to ask questions. Consumed with guilt, MJ confessed.

Her mother, single now after her father left for work one day and never returned, insisted she go to Father Garcia, confess her cardinal sin and pray for forgiveness.

***

"You slut!" her mother had screamed. "You little slut! I knew I couldn't trust you! Who's the father? Or can't you even tell me that!?

MJ remembered the horror as if it was yesterday. She had been nauseous every morning for ages but hid it from her mother by vomiting in the cornfield on the way to school. A first-class student, her grades had slipped.

When she failed her first, and then her second and third exam, Mr. Sutherland, her homeroom teacher, insisted on meeting with her mother. These marks did not reflect the MJ he knew. Something was wrong.

Meanwhile, she avoided Alex like the plague. He couldn't understand what had happened between them. It was only yesterday they had pledged their futures with one another.

MJ knew her mother could not stand to be in the same house with her daughter after her pregnancy was confirmed. She overheard her on the phone. Frantically looking for a 'home' far away for unwed mothers.

And so, MJ had left smalltown Brighton, Ontario for Toronto to stay with "Aunt Betsy" for awhile. She needed to recover from increased anxiety and depression brought on by the abandonment of her father.

She heard later that her mother received mountains of pity from the community after losing both her husband and her daughter. The poor woman. It was enough to drive anyone crazy. Her well-meaning but nosy neighbours heaped praise and sympathy on her.

Meanwhile, MJ had been forced to accept a fake first name -- Hope -- when she entered the Home for Unwed Mothers. She was deemed a pitiable example of a girl gone astray with loose morals and a need for a strong Christian faith.

She had been forced to work at household chores to help pay for expenses incurred during her confinement. The charity in charge strongly advised her to give up her baby after delivery, the best solution for both baby and mother. When she did, and of course the Superior insisted she must, MJ/Hope was warned not to try and find her baby nor look for the adoptive parents, if any.

In other words, nine months of MJ's life -- and her baby -- had to be erased from her memory. The pregnancy and birth had never happened.

But, of course, both did happen. The baby hole in her heart took seed and grew instantly.

And MJ vowed she would find her daughter come hell or high water.

Chapter Two

1979

MJ sat alone in her midnight blue Mazda 3 under the harsh parking lot light of the SuperCentre. She stared bleakly ahead out the windshield.

Even from a distance, she could see flares from the industrial smokestacks, flames leaping into the March twilight sky. Reminding her of her grim existence in this small mill town of Brighton.

Bagged groceries, just tucked into the trunk, meant she had no real excuse to leave the house for at least another week.

Except for her librarian job. A position that had created a lifeline to the real world. Introduced her to real people and real lives and real information that Tommy had denied her as he kept her prisoner.

She had had no access to a computer. Had no idea of the wealth of information available at her fingertips on the worldwide web.

Fortunately, library resources had allowed her access, introducing this other world of self-education. Self-reliance. Self-confidence.

And re-introduced her to Alex.

Most importantly, the library had provided the possibility she might find a clue leading to her daughter. At long last. Her baby given up against her will. MJ could still feel -- inhale -- the sweet fragrance from the tiny wriggling bundle in her arms.

Each morning when she awoke and each evening before she fell asleep, she rubbed her stomach to relieve the familiar baby hole ache that was forever part of her heart and psyche. *Maya.*

As she day-dreamed in the car, feeling guilty because she might be late getting home, her idle mind began playing with the ever-present question: how to leave Tommy? To begin her quest? Start over again?

For as long as she could remember living this upside-down, inside-out relationship with Tommy, she had known her only way to sanity and a normal life was to run away. But where? How?

Psychologically, she feared Tommy but her heart remembered his sweet side, too. When everyone, including her mother, had forsaken her, ignored this unwed teenaged mother, it was Tommy who took her in. Licked her wounds. Helped her heal. He had been good to her.

But that was a long time ago. And the rescue had come at a hefty price. Her freedom. She felt like a butterfly caught in a large net that allowed her to live but with clipped wings.

Tommy was still her master. She was his hostage. He was her constant protector against the world. But, like a fledgling bird ready to leave the nest, she wanted out.

MJ bit her lip. She thought about her wasted life up to this point. From a typical loving-life teenager to a 40-year-old captive woman, she had been controlled by this dominant man who still held power over her. Whom she had trouble leaving.

How did she get trapped into this really bad relationship? She'd read about the Stockholm Syndrome and the more she thought about it, the more MJ concluded she was a living example of that sick mental disorder.

It had taken her how many years? About 24 to edge her way back towards normalcy! To decide she was a human being with her own wants and needs.

She longed to be free. From Tommy and his moods and his threat of physical abuse. And his dominant love and intimacy that kept her imprisoned year after year after year. Fear of his brutality, his threat to hunt her down. Kill her if necessary. She shivered.

But I'm stronger now. Finally. This time it's going to happen. I am leaving. For me. For Maya.

Then reality set in. *Now I need a plan.*

Chapter Three

Still daydreaming in the Mazda in the SuperCentre parking lot, she sighed. Mentally relived her day.

At home that morning, MJ had stood in the shower stall luxuriating in the fragrance of L'Occidente's foaming lavender-scented gel. Mentally making escape plans. When she stepped onto the oval black cotton bath mat, she heard him.

"MJ!"

Tommy.

"Where are you?" he thundered.

"Here," she raised her voice a little.

Heard his clumping upstairs, into their bedroom. She also smelled burnt toast wafting up from the kitchen. This meant he would be in a foul mood.

"For Chrissake, couldn't you have been more helpful?"

I am so not wanting to be here, MJ told herself. To Tommy she said, "what is it you want?

Or need?" She had heard the taunt in her voice, aching for an argument.

"What the hell's gotten into you, lady?" he suddenly bellowed. Tommy could be mistaken for a boxer. At least once upon a time. His muscles were softer now. His blue grey eyes smoked with anger. She watched his trimmed goatee move up and down, like a wooden puppet's mouth, as he spoke. She knew he was ready for her derision. Since his psychology degree all those years ago, she knew he thought how best to handle her.

"You're always yelling… know that?" she countered.

"Maybe I wouldn't if you treated me a little better." He took one look at her wet body then cooed in a more civilized manner, "well, you could've told me you were taking a shower. You smell good. Come here to your man, baby."

"Don't touch me!" she challenged. "I'm in no mood…."

"You're never in the right mood lately, damn it woman. Don't worry… later." He winked. Chuckling loudly, he had retreated downstairs. No explanation why he had called her in the first place. "I like a chick with attitude," he yelled back.

Probably checking up on me, she thought bitterly, then smiled, pleased at her reflection. *Soon I won't have to put up with him.*

Towelling herself dry, Mary Jane took a critical look at the woman standing before the full-length bedroom mirror. At 40, she decided she wasn't bad looking. She wasn't a beauty but she could still turn heads. Wrinkling her turned-up nose, she studied her emerald green eyes under a tousled crown of copper curls. Her eyes had moved critically over her body: still firm breasts, narrow waist, a patch of curly copper hair between her long legs; slender ankles.

In the end, she decided she was well put together. Ready to step back out into the world. Alone. To follow her quest. To find her baby. Her 24-year-old baby.

What made her think her daughter would want to see her? As always, she had pushed that awful thought to the back of her mind. Brought herself back to the present. Stared at the industrial flames in the distance.

Blinking. she thought about her Escape. Brave? Suicidal? Crazy? Leave everything behind? Without Tommy, without the scars of her youth, she might have a chance at a rewarding and exciting new life. And she had a purpose. A burning goal. Find Maya.

***

Still reflecting alone in her car – grateful for the time alone -- she ruminated about the serendipity of working at the local town library. Glenda, the head librarian, had been a godsend. It was Glenda who introduced her to classic literature. But it was through her love of the printed word that MJ became self-educated. More self-confident.

21

There was still much of a timid woman inside her. Tommy liked that yielding goddess role. MJ played it for his benefit but beneath her soft exterior a wiser, harder, sharper woman had been evolving, looking for an escape route.

All through her captive years, books had been MJ's salvation. Through reading and observation, she had studied self-therapy. She decided to carefully keep up the helpless damsel role for a little while longer so Tommy would not detect any major change in her personality.

While her mind lingered on her unknown future, she once again stared ahead at the mesmerizing industrial flames licking the darkening sky.

Suddenly, a sharp tap at her car window broke her reverie.

Gasping in fear, she turned to see a face.

Chapter Four

Heart beating wildly, she stared, then smiled at the man peering into the window.

"Alex…hi," she smiled warmly as she opened the window. "You scared me."

"Just checking you're ok, MJ. Saw you sitting in a dream state."

"I am in a dream state, Alex."

He nodded, straightened. "Maybe you'd like a dream coffee with me before heading home?"

"Sounds perfect. Let's head to Timmy's over there. I'll follow."

He nodded. Returned to his car.

Alex, thought MJ. Her childhood sweetheart who had been innocently responsible for those ghastly visits to Father Garcia so long ago. Now why didn't I think of him before?

Sitting in Tim Horton's, she realized how much she needed this cup of steaming dark-roasted coffee. The deep aroma charged her senses. Alex changed his mind, opted for a hot chocolate instead. She breathed in the comforting aroma as he brought the mug to his mouth. His mouth had always been inviting, she thought.

"How's it goin'?" His friendly blue eyes smiled at her. Despite the years, MJ decided Alex turned out exactly as she knew he would. Small town boy, owner of his smalltown business. A model citizen. She wondered if he ever remembered their tryst in the cornfield that led her to where she was today. Interestingly, she mused, he never married.

"You mean at the library?" She looked at him across the formica-topped table in this brightly-lit coffee shop. Curly chestnut-coloured hair fell over his forehead, giving him a cherub look. His face was pleasant, meaning he looked like the boy-next-door in a thousand films. No-one would notice him. Except when he started talking and his eyes crinkled and he made you feel like the only person in the world.

"Yeah. Of course, I mean the library. When I was there yesterday, you were glued to the screen."

MJ grunted her acknowledgement. "Was reading an article about a girl who might be -- but probably isn't -- my daughter."

"MJ…" Alex's blue eyes softened. His brows furrowed. "That was such a long time ago. I know you've suffered but you have to be realistic, too. You're married…"

"I'm not, Alex. You know that." She watched his eyes smile. "Tommy and I never married. He's kept me captive all these years cuz he figures I don't have enough money --- or guts --- to leave him."

She sipped her coffee. Alex drank his hot chocolate. She looked again into those clear blue receptive eyes. Smiled.

During the times they had spent together in the library -- ostensibly searching for real estate deals so he could expand his men's clothing store into the county -- they had once more developed a close rapport. Reconnected. Slowly, MJ had shared her full story with Alex. She had assumed everyone in town knew her disgraced past. And she learned, too, that his present fortune began in the roots of his long-time and respected local merchant family.

As they researched in the library together, he had asked about her past after she left town. Said he never heard anything.

"Well, bad girl that I was, I had an illegitimate daughter out of town who was quickly adopted. I returned penniless and homeless." She had stopped. Looked down. Ashamed to face him.

She continued. "And it was Tommy who took me in. No questions asked. I was so young and vulnerable then. Didn't realize he was using me for his own needs."

Now facing Alex in Timmy's, MJ saw him glance at his wrist-watch. As if time with her was clocked. When she asked, he nervously admitted that Tommy's reputation for attacking any male who paid attention to her was well known in town.

MJ knew this. It was part of Tommy's scheme to keep her available only to him.

Helplessly, she watched Alex gulp more of his hot chocolate, then heard him ask: "Why don't you leave him, MJ?" His fingers played nervously on the table. He picked up his spoon, swirling it lazily in the air.

Her green eyes clouded. "I'm getting closer to that day, Alex, believe me."

She lowered her head. Glanced around the coffee shop at the local townspeople. Recognized no-one. Sighed. Looked at Alex as she drained her coffee cup. Said quietly, "I better go before he comes looking…"

"And I better get back to the store…we're getting ready for a sale," he quickly countered.

As MJ pushed herself up from the table, he covered his warm hand firmly but gently over hers.

"MJ," he said. "I never forgot us. Remember I'm here for you."

She bit her lip. Then whispered, almost laughing hysterically, "Would you drive me to Mexico, Alex? Would you take a chance and run away from this god-forsaken town with me?"

His bright blue eyes connected with her beseeching green ones so intensely that both felt the electric charge between them. She gasped when she saw him nod.

Silently, he mouthed 'tomorrow we'll talk.'

Oh, be still my beating heart, prayed MJ.

Chapter Five

Back in the Mazda, after that burning eye exchange with Alex, MJ slowed down her breathing and sat silently. Thinking again.

Could Alex really be her ticket out of town? Would he actually help her leave? She was getting braver at handling Tommy. She almost fell off her chair the other night when he had proposed marriage. That in itself was a telltale signal. He must be feeling she might run off. That obviously she was feeling stronger. More self-reliant.

Her wary eyes scanned the landscape of nearby fast-food outlets. There was Tim Horton's. Of course. Then her eyes drifted to Mexican Burritos. Funny, she thought, her ideas of Mexico had nothing to do with burritos although…

…Mexico had been calling her name for a long time. From a resort vacation in Cancun long ago when she was still under Tommy's spell and he had treated her like a goddess and not a caged bird, she fell in love with the history, mystery and wisdom of the ancient Maya civilization. Indeed, she had found it a curious coincidence that she had named her baby, Maya, long before visiting Mexico.

So, her pull to Maya country was incredibly strong, especially the Yucatán Peninsula. And, as if to endorse that attraction, she had received support from the unlikeliest of people.

Glenda, the head librarian, had mentioned a friend who worked in an English speaking library somewhere in that Mexican state. Because of her connections in the area, Glenda had even proposed to the town's library board that this small-town library could specialize in Maya history. Make the library renowned in southwestern Ontario. Maybe even offer Spanish lessons. After all, Spanish ranked above French as a popular world language. Glenda had aspirations of making the town library a worthy attraction because of a specialty. Who knows where this could lead, she suggested to the board? Maybe wealthy Spanish patrons would support a cross-cultural program. She was almost obsessed with these possibilities.

Especially after she'd read an online article at the library. *Canadian Woman Founds Maya Eco-retreat for Tourists.* The story described how a young Canadian woman, Selene Rupert, age 24, was helping to build Maya-style replica *casas* for tourist rentals so visitors could "more fully experience the nearby archeological site of Ek Balaam" in an ecologically friendly environment.

"Look at this article!" Glenda had pointed out to MJ who was cataloguing in the reference department at the time. Glenda, with her shoulder length dark brown hair and round-rimmed glasses, always created a misty shroud of roses from her cologne whenever she moved through the library. She was also one of the few in whom MJ had confided and now, as a show of support, Glenda often drew Maya online items to MJ's attention.

After she'd read the article, MJ's heart had skipped a beat. Was she stretching her imagination? She had stared at, studied, the photograph of the young woman developer accompanying the article. Whispered *"Maya"* slowly, reverently. Could this girl possibly be her missing daughter? The one she'd been trying to find forever? She sighed. She was probably grasping at straws again.

Maya was the name she'd given her daughter at birth. 24 years ago! She had begged a sympathetic nurse to ask her adoptive parents to please keep the name. Removed from her mother's arms two days after birth, Maya was MJ's only reason for living. She could still remember her unforgettable baby sweet scent, feel her soft, perfect skin. From the moment she had heard her baby cry and then lost her so abruptly, MJ had carried that baby hole, like an open wound, in her heart.

MJ studied Selene Rupert's photo on the computer screen. What made her jolt even more was the age: 24. Her missing daughter was 24. But even in her wildest moments, MJ recognized there were many 24-year-old women in the world! Even in Mexico.

Staring at the image, she wondered, does she look like me? This Selene's hair looked dark. What colour were her eyes? Tough to tell in a grainy reproduced newspaper shot. She recalled other dead ends in her online search for Maya. She'd been crushed each time she found a Maya looking for her birth mother. There was one in Toronto but her European background ruled that out.

Back to reality in her parked car, she shifted her green eyes to the flares in the distance while the early years of anguish flashed like fires intermittently in her mind. She never realized memories could remain so vivid. Now 40, those long-ago torments still felt as raw as when she was 16.

That terrible, vivid memory. MJ's rapist -- Maya's father -- was none other than a respected priest. She could easily have identified him at the time as the creep who betrayed her trust in him. But no-one would have believed her, of course, so she had remained silent. After all, a pregnant unwed 16-year-old was in enough trouble already.

****

Slowly driving out of the parking lot, MJ's mind began to wander -- for the thousandth time -- to her missing baby.

She'd held that beautiful sleeping bundle with the dark, wet hair in her arms so briefly after her delivery. Instant bonding. Carefully she had unwrapped the pink blanket to study her baby's perfect little body. Five tiny fingers on each tiny hand. Five tiny toes on each tiny foot. The tiniest of fingernails and toenails. Slowly, gently, humbly, she remembered turning her beautiful daughter over so the front of her perfect little body rested comfortably, naturally, across MJ's still-swollen belly.

That's when she had seen it. The birthmark. Small. Round. Flat. Dark brown. At the bottom of her baby's spine. Its appearance had been a surprise. But she had determined it was something she would always remember when she started looking for her. For, without a doubt, she was going to find her daughter. If it took the rest of her life, she was going to find Maya and explain to her what happened, and that she, her mother, had always loved her, wanted her…

It took only one efficient nurse to gently but firmly lift Maya from her arms. Whisked her away so the separation had been as deft as a surgeon's scalpel. Adoptive parents had been ready, waiting.

She learned later the parents were a professional couple: he, a medical doctor, she, a physiotherapist, from nearby Ottawa. But no other information. Through blinding tears and heaving sobs, she had signed papers. Signed away her daughter. The only consolation had been Maya's parents were professional. That would mean her daughter would have better opportunities in life.

What an idiot I was! MJ muttered, massaging that aching baby hole in her heart.

She had begun her mourning the instant she gave up her daughter. She had grieved for her all these years. Now she had only one purpose in life. Find Maya.

***

Much later, with her daughter ever foremost in her mind, MJ had researched birthmarks. She had always assumed the birthmark at the bottom of the spine meant a Mongolian Spot. Which made no sense in her case unless the raping priest was Asian: although he was -- she had remembered frowning at the realization -- from Mexico. Rev. Garcia had been on a cultural exchange.

Intrigued, MJ discovered once she began studying the Maya world that her daughter's birthmark location was common among Maya people of the Yucatán Peninsula. The mark was referred to as *Wa,* meaning 'circle' in Maya.

Once she made that connection, MJ convinced herself Maya would follow a spiritual path to study, or live, among the Maya. So certain was this feeling in her bones, she decided if she couldn't find her daughter in Canada, she had every reason to believe Maya might already be in Maya Mexico. Or was she being foolish? After years of searching, what made her think Maya would really be in Mexico?

And now there was this online article. She needed more information.

She'd already tried googling this young Canadian entrepreneur with not much luck. Only the article Glenda had pointed out kept coming up.

MJ was determined to connect with this Selene Rupert. Even if it meant running to Mexico.

And she knew now -- as certain as she was heading to that country south of the United States -- that Alex would be with her. His last words were *let's talk tomorrow. Let's just do it before we start thinking about reasons why we can't.*

Chapter Six

Selene woke up alone -- and nude -- in her favourite *cabaña* in her eco-retreat tucked inland from Yucatán's Gulf of Mexico coastline.

She stretched, leapt out of bed onto the turquoise natural sisal carpet with the Maya Corn God design, and padded out the door to the attached ecologically designed bathroom: solar heated outdoor shower with electric backup and a dehydrating compost toilet.

Tossing her long curly mahogany-coloured mane out of her hazel-coloured eyes, she studied herself in the mirror: she liked her large golden hoop earrings and the small diamond stud on the left side of her nose. Made her feel exotic.

She smiled wryly as she recalled her drunken state on that long ago day when she had *Man N'enex* -- the Maya word for *welcome* -- tattooed above her tailbone. Just above her birthmark. The tat had been the only reminder of her alcoholic haze days. And she didn't mind this one memory. Ever since, she had felt an affinity with the Maya.

Pulling back her luxurious hair into a ponytail, she mused how she'd come a long way from the booze-filled days she had shared with Mike: her business partner/sometime lover.

Silently thanking the Maya gods for good health and good vibes, she grabbed her bikini off the locally handcrafted sisal chair for her morning swim.

In the background, she heard squawking green parrots in flight from a palm tree to another taller one. She sipped her cool aloe drink from the mini fridge. Then opened the wooden door of her oval cabaña to the brilliant Yucatecan sunshine, her eyes feasting on palm-fringed trees and lush tropical foliage ringing the pool.

"You've come a long way, baby," she murmured appreciatively, approaching the turquoise waters of her natural swimming pool. Due to Mike's eco knowledge, the manmade cenote-like pool was bio-filtered with a minimum use of chemicals and filled by tapping into the system of pristine underground river water 40 meters below.

Glancing around, she didn't see Mike. He must be running along the beach, she surmised, his usual early morning jog in the nearby small fishing town of Progreso. Not far from their eco-retreat.

Swimming long, rhythmic strokes in her pool, she was pleased this was the tourist off-season. No responsibilities and the pool to herself.

Her mind meandered hazily and came to rest on her parents. She must FaceTime them soon again, let them know she was okay. She tried to connect every two weeks or so which sometimes proved difficult at first: her boozing habit; and now: her busyness with the eco-retreat. Whenever she did, she realized she was slipping farther and farther away from life in Canada. Her mother, always sad, sometimes weepy, cajoled: "why don't you come home, Selene?"

Her father always appeared angry. He had this furrow in his forehead between his eyebrows that used to disappear when he smiled but now was a permanent feature of his facial expression. Whether he was happy, sad or indifferent, her father's face showed this constant furrow. So, he always looked displeased.

No matter what, Selene knew she owed her parents an explanation for running off to Mexico. She smiled sardonically. That sounded so dramatic. Still, she did worry about her father. She knew he'd been having heart problems and there was a definite wheeze in his voice when they chatted. Somehow, she knew her mother would always be okay no matter what happened. She tended to be a drama queen. Like Selene.

So, Selene, she said to herself, *be honest with them. Tell them your plans. They deserve to know. Invite them here. They'd probably be very proud of your accomplishments. Then they'd accept your choices and get off your back. Maybe they could all be friends again. Like long before she disappeared with Mike.*

Brushing her long, curly, dark auburn hair, she couldn't help thinking about how she got here from there.

Chapter Seven

Four years ago, after she and Mike had decided to remain in Puerto Progreso, Selene had come to a sad but stark conclusion: *I'm wasting my life with this guy. We drink too much with other expats who rely too much on booze from morning til night and... I'm afraid I'm going to wake up one day at 50 and still be here. Alone. In a vegetative state. I haven't studied the Maya like I planned. My reason for coming with Mike. Or done anything constructive. Just drink.*

This morbid thought kept reappearing in her thoughts. Which led to a vindictive verbal exchange with Mike.

"You're nothing but a drunk, Selene," he'd accused. "You blame me and everyone else. But it's only you who can change." And he turned his back on her while she scratched his bare skin with her long fingernails until it bled, screaming it had been all his fault.

When she had exhausted her tears, and Mike had pushed her down on the bed before storming out of their *departamento*, Selene had sobbed herself to sleep.

But not before her tortured mind had replayed how alcohol had taken over her life.

She remembered, if she was brutally honest, the abuse began years ago when she was about 16.

That's when, like other teens her age, she felt insecure and way too overprotected. Ugly. Stupid. She suffered intense crushes on most of the senior boys' basketball team. Because she knew they weren't interested in her, she felt safe. An ardent admirer from afar.

But all that had changed quickly. After one particular late-night party.

Her father, a successful physician catering to the wealthy, had gone to great lengths to bring up his only daughter in a large modern home on the edge of the city's diplomatic residences in Earnscliffe Park. Her mother, a professional physiotherapist, enjoyed a side business with this privileged set.

It was Selene's long-time friend, Sandra, who unwittingly had changed her life. Sandra casually offered her the invitation: "After the championship game. Sue's having an open house at her place. Her parents are gone for the weekend. All the hot team guys will be there."

"Not sure my parents will be okay with that."

"Don't tell them, silly! Tell them you're staying with me overnight at my house."

"What happens if they call your house and I'm not there?"

Sandra had all the answers. "You have a cellphone…use it to check in with them."

And that's how Selene found herself at an all-night drunken spree. Complete with towering senior basketball team guys roaming around the large executive home. So innocent was she that her life experience to this point involved limited alcohol use. At Sue's, she sipped her first taste of beer and decided against it. After finishing the bottle, she opted to drink red wine; she had enjoyed a cabernet sauvignon on special occasions at home with her parents.

Everyone at the party was on the prowl. A mellow Eagles hit overpowered the chatter, hardly recognizable because of the noise level. Clinking bottles and glasses and shrieks of hysterical laughter reverberated throughout the finely furnished home. Later in the evening, lights were dimmed. A few party-goers left. Some just made it outside before vomiting. As drinking elevated, so, too, did the groping and sexual innuendo.

At first shy and withdrawn, Selene discovered that wine liberated her senses. She enjoyed the buzz, the light-headed bravado that came along with the booze.

When Bob, one of her basketball team crushes cruised by, Selene caught his eye. His tipsy smile and wide blue eyes followed her as she melted into the woodwork. Literally. She opted to hide by the long spiral wooden staircase. Beside a giant potted palm.

"Hi," he said, clumsily spilling the beer from his mug.

"Hi," she whispered in awe. She was talking to one of her idols and her heart wouldn't let her forget it!

"Haven't seen you at one of these parties before."

"Haven't been to one before that's why." She had to get close to him to read his lips. In the low light and loud background music, her hearing suffered.

"Wanna find a quiet space to talk?" he grinned.

"Sure."

"Let's try a room upstairs."

A silent warning bell sounded inside her. As did her wildly beating heart. Bob, the team captain, was paying attention to her!

Like a compliant child, she followed him up the thickly carpeted stairs. He opened the first door on the right. Faint light made it difficult to see. Except it was easy to spot a couple of bodies writhing together on the double bed.

"Whoops! Sorry...." He offered to no-one in particular. Especially not the couple in bed.

"Close the damn door," came the male order. "We're busy." A female giggle.

"Let's try this one." Bob turned the door knob on another room down the hall. "Ah," he said.

"Empty. Come inside my beautiful miss…..?" he paused…

"Selene," she half-whispered in fear and heightened arousal.

"Miss Selene. Perfect name for a perfect lady." And he led her inside, closed the door, sat on the bed, patted the place beside him. "For you," he smiled. "Sit, Miss Selene."

Captivated, insides crawling with desire, Selene did as she was told.

"Now," said Bob gently. "You know who I am but I don't know who you are. Tell me all about you, Miss Marvelous Selene."

With fire coursing through her veins, she started to talk. Stammer really.

Somehow, he stopped her murmurs with sloppy wet kisses. In her mouth. Around her mouth. Back of her neck. She could taste, smell his beer breath. Then he took her hand, guided it to his hard penis, erect through his jeans. Lay her on her back.

Selene gasped.

Like a wild animal, he bent over her, rubbing his crotch against her prone body.

"You like that?" he nudged her up and down her face and into her tangled mahogany-tinted hair. "Feel good? Want to touch it?"

Stunned. She couldn't answer.

He unzipped and out it sprang. Stiff. Moist. Ready.

"Now let's not do anything stupid, Miss Selene," he panted running his fingers through strands of her hair. Stroking her face. "No fucking. No troubles…"

She almost collapsed with relief.

"…just suck til I cum…then swallow it, babe…"

Much later, Selene realized how lucky she was. He didn't care about pleasing her. He only wanted her to please him. At this most astonishing moment, stroking his hard cock while he groaned with pleasure, she thought sex and alcohol were a great mix. As far as she was concerned, she was still a virgin.

And, after the encounter, when Bob bumped into her in the halls at high school, or spied her in the bleachers at a basketball game, he had nodded -- only very slightly -- in her direction. As if acknowledging her was painful. As if she was barely visible.

***

Looking back, it had been damn hard to recover from alcoholism on her own but she did it and in doing so, she had regained Mike's respect. And her own.

The day, in their *departamento* she actually prepared dinner for them both -- an old-fashioned roast chicken miraculously perfected in a Mexican gas oven while he mashed potatoes from the people's *mercado* -- Mike acknowledged that maybe she was on the way to booze-free living.

It helped she had developed another passionate interest, too. Her fascination with all things Maya had led her to the inland state capital city of Mérida, a half hour bus ride away. There, she had sought out the LES: Library for English Speakers. Selene was thrilled when Bonnie, the Head Librarian, tapped into her Maya history interest. Recognizing her zeal, Bonnie invited Selene to assist in developing a special Maya section in the LES. Selene inhaled the offer.

That infamous roast chicken dinner (never repeated again!) plus her fascination with LES, led Mike to listen earnestly to her frustrations, her plans. Because she sensed part of him still cared for her, she took his comment to heart: *Maybe having your dream incomplete is what's driven you to drink.*

The longtime bond between them led to the commitment from Mike that had eluded her up to now: it was time to create their dream eco-retreat together. It was easy to live cheaply here. When they sat down with paper and pencil, they were pleasantly surprised. Their savings in Canada: his from a prior summer construction job, hers from her parents' generous allowance, had increased in value through strategic investments by her father. Land was cheap here. Especially inland, away from the beach. Time to get back to why the Yucatán held this magic spell over them both.

From the first time she saw the distinct Maya oval homes from the back of Mike's motorbike, Selene fell in love with the picturesque *casas* of thatched roofs and walls of clay and straw, perfect for the hot climate. They reminded her of cocoons. Cozy. Protective.

Later, she and Mike discovered these sturdy oval-shaped casas were sustainable and sensible for this Yucatecan climate. In these days of green-conscience living, she was sure they could make a go of an eco-retreat based on how the Maya lived in the past.

And now their dream was becoming a reality.

***

Watching the sun rise over the eco-retreat, Selene recalled hers and Mike's first encounter with Progreso, the rundown grungy fishing village on the Gulf of Mexico coast: dirty, dusty, empty lots strewn with smelly garbage *(basura),* gravel streets strewn with prostrate stray thin dogs. Her first impulse was to keep on rolling down the highway. She marvelled that they had actually stopped here.

Thinking back, Selene couldn't believe they had driven into this dilapidated place on Mike's motorbike after a cool 6000 km/3750 mile ride from Ottawa, Canada. Four long years -- and many adventures -- ago. Both escaping the plebeian lifestyle offered to Carleton University graduates. Mike, a small-town guy from Brighton just outside of Ottawa, and Selene, daughter of a wealthy professional couple, joined unlikely forces to forge new horizons.

Tired and hungry, they had looked around for a place to rent in this poverty-stricken town. Lots of empty *casas*.

They wheeled around and took a good look at an upper-level apartment with its two-colour decorating scheme of white and turquoise. One large bedroom, complete with hammock hooks, faced the sea.

Two shuttered windows along the rear wall opened to a sandy backyard ringed with brilliant hues of rose, purple, and pink bougainvillea. The apartment was actually one large room: a tiny kitchen and *baño* and separately, the master bedroom, with hammock hooks. The décor was nautical: fish and shells, driftwood, bright bird and sea photos.

"The price is right," Mike said. So, they rented it on the spot. Four years ago.

*****

And now, they had joined forces and actually built an eco-retreat on the outskirts of town. Surveying the skyline from the newly-built retreat, Selene embraced the sunshine. Hot even at this early hour of 8 a.m.

Lifting her head to the cobalt blue sky with its brilliant golden orb rising higher, she watched a V-shaped line of pelicans sail in perfect unison towards the sea.

Today, life was perfect. She could even envisage her future. A financially successful eco-retreat in this land of sunshine and tamales. Maybe with Mike.

Selene could not know then how her life would change.

Chapter Eight

During the one-hour drive in his Jeep to his latest out-of-town job, Tommy obsessed about MJ.

A successful carpenter, he enjoyed creating beautifully carved and crafted pieces of woodwork. Often using reclaimed wood from surrounding farms. Today, though, he was not thinking beautiful. He was feeling uneasy, queasy. He was always suspicious when it came to *her.* Feared someday she'd disappear.

Things were not going well on the home front. He felt MJ's distance. That she wasn't with him anymore. And he didn't like it. Didn't like the work she'd been doing at the library. Felt his current life foundation slipping away. All because of her. His reasons for keeping her suppressed, under his wing all these years, were personal. Related to his own insecurities, he knew.

And yes, there was the matter of his cruel streak. A psych grad from Western, he had tried to understand himself. But not too hard. Because he couldn't resist the power of fear. Because he had been a victim as an undergrad, he reconciled that he really wasn't responsible for his actions. Victim impact and all that.

But, thinking back to MJ, Tommy knew change was inevitable.

She had blossomed from an immature, afraid-of-her-shadow teenager, to an attractive, mature and somewhat self-assured woman. Fear of him had diminished but not totally disappeared. He knew she pretended to make love with him now. Pacified him. Agreed with him. Gone was the grateful kitten eager to please her master. In its place, a bored lioness. Bad combination, he figured.

One fact he did know. She couldn't go very far. No money. No real friends. Only started earning a little when he allowed her to work at the library. Piss on that place and the head librarian! That Glenda bitch had introduced her to all kinds of possibilities. MJ soon figured out what she had been missing. Worse, she'd gotten all gung-ho on this Maya stuff. Even believed her daughter from the priest-rape was there! God help us, he swore, nothing makes sense anymore.

Back in his university days, he vowed never to return to this dumpy little town of Brighton. But, again, that was before *it* happened. *It* was his victimization from a brutal sex abuse attack during a frat initiation. His gut still upchucked until he quickly suppressed the horror, pushed it back down inside his dark soul. After the attack, all he wanted was home in safe, quiet, boring smalltown Ontario. Where minions still debated the weather and whether Spring planting would be early or late.

But his mind wouldn't, couldn't forget. He kept returning to that defining experience, reliving the horror and shame as if it had just happened.

Now, feeling insecure and a bit lost, he reflected again on his need to conquer and capture MJ. Once upon a time he was not so controlling or

-- and he hesitated to admit this -- cruel. He knew, though, the change had come at university. When he had been such a blithe and naïve freshman idiot.

When he was alone, Tommy cringed at the nightmare memory: how he had been lured by seniors to the frat house. How they had plied him with alcohol while pretending to like him. How he had stupidly, childishly, trusted them. How they had pushed him into a dark closet and locked the door after he dumbly admitted his biggest fear was claustrophobia. How they had stood on the other side of the door taunting him. Made him promise to perform vile sex acts in return for an unlocked door.

Once free of the closet, Tommy had been violently attacked: repeatedly raped, even with the neck of a beer bottle. He later mentally relived the horror scene. Nausea, vomiting, blood everywhere. After that fiasco, he vowed to always control his emotions. Never reveal his inner thoughts.

The other problem was -- and Tommy knew this -- his abusive sex experience had unleashed some very bad demons of his own. He bullied. Taunted. Inhaled rough sex. Holding a female captive all these years stimulated his deepest animal desires. As much as he liked to use his hands to create beautiful works with wood, he knew he could also use them to destroy pretty things. Like MJ.

After a dinner of his famous (by his standards) barbeque ribs last night, when Tommy had had too much to drink and was feeling self-confident and indestructible, he suddenly blurted out something he'd been thinking about lately.

"How 'bout we get married, MJ? We could even go on a honeymoon together! Like hot babes ready to devour each other."

He was stunned, totally unprepared, for her ho-hum response as she sat with her back to him drinking coffee, staring out the large back picture window in their kitchen that overlooked a ravine. "Not the right time, Tommy…"

Later that night in bed, still in shock by her lack of enthusiasm for his impromptu proposal, he attempted to arouse her. He wanted hot sex. Needed it desperately to re-establish his dominance.

It didn't take long before his fears went from bad to worse. Tommy had sensed something was terribly out of sync. MJ didn't 'feel' like any rough sex, she said. She was tired, she said. And when he had plunged himself deep inside her and lost control, he knew she had faked her climax. Something was going on in MJ's life and he needed, wanted desperately, to know what it was.

Before finally falling asleep, he decided it was time to talk things over with cousin Copley. He almost snorted with derision. Big, bad Tommy confessing his shortcomings with the stick-thin Copley, he of the round owl glasses, stringy blonde hair and openly gay lover: an unlikely scenario if ever there was one!

But Cop also had a level head on his shoulders. And he knew all about Tommy's big bad side: the terrifying side Tommy had difficulty keeping in check.

Chapter Nine

Although she had 'officially' stopped drinking, Selene soon realized she still liked a buzz every once in a while. The key was moderation. She just wasn't living in an alcoholic haze anymore, she reasoned.

When she drank a little too much, she became unrealistically melancholy about the simple but harsh life surrounding her in this part of the Yucatán, particularly among citizens of the nearby fishing town. She fondly recalled some of the characters -- and their unforgiving lives -- she and Mike had encountered while on motorbike.

Like the clown.

At one of Progreso's five traffic lights, a lone clown waited on the corner for the red-light signal. Once it changed, he whipped out quickly in front of the stopped traffic, juggling four balls high in the air and up behind his back. Never dropped a ball. His was serious business. He juggled to collect *pesos* from captive motorists stopped at the light.

From a distance the clown looked cheerful, a big red painted smile across his mouth. His nose was covered with a red bulb, his face painted white with red round defined circles on his cheeks. A faded black felt top hat sat jauntily on his head. His outfit, once bright colours in squares of green and blue, was frayed and tattered. Worn running shoes with escaping toes semi-covered his feet.

Selene studied this sad clown trying to look happy as he juggled by their idling motorbike. Always the same young man in the same outfit. His real mouth was forlorn. As he juggled, his dark eyes darted to and fro, from Selene to Mike and back to Selene again. He looked for some spark of interest or encouragement, some recognition from his audience that meant he will earn pesos before moving on to the stopped car behind them.

Selene always kept a few extra pesos in her pockets for the clown. When she dropped the coins into his hat, he did not look at them. Instead, after muttering a quick *gracias,* he looked deep into her hazel-coloured eyes, almost hypnotizing her with his deep chocolate ones.

"Tu nombre?" she asked quickly.

"Carlos," he answered, before rushing to collect more from the following car while the traffic light was still red.

The next time Selene ran into Carlos, she didn't recognize him. Walking along Calle 80, Progreso's main street, her mind focused on getting to the *tortilleria,* she accidentally bumped into a serious-looking young man. His height was the same as hers, 5'6". Her hazel eyes locked into his darker ones.

"Perdóname," she mumbled.

"It is Carlos," he said. His dark eyes held hers.

Selene looked again. Studied the serious chocolate eyes, soon recognizing the traffic clown out of costume.

"Carlos!" she murmured.

"Y tu nombre?" he asked, smiling. Not in a hurry now.

"Selene." She smiled back. *"Hablas ingles?"*

"Un poquito. A little." He stood there, holding her captive on the street with his serious eyes.

"Coffee?" she finally asked, mesmerized. She pointed to a nearby shop.

"Si, por favor."

Walking side by side on the uneven pavement of the sidewalk, carefully stepping around the short Maya women vendors selling their vegetables carefully stacked in pyramids along the street, they reached the open-air corner coffee shop. Sat side-by-side at an empty table facing the street as the aroma of freshly-roasted Mexican coffee tantalized their senses.

Selene enjoyed Carlos. Out of costume, he was witty. Captivated her with his halting English. He asked her many questions. Where was she from? Why live here? She explained – slowly so he could understand -- how she and Mike were working on opening an eco-retreat for tourists. Part of the plan was to teach foreigners about this part of Mexico, its history and Maya heritage.

In turn, Selene learned Carlos was the eldest of four brothers. He had been accepted into the state Teachers' College. But that was before his father, a fisherman and sole family wage earner, had left in his small boat early one morning for his daily catch. A nasty, unexpected storm had brewed far out in The Gulf catching many of the seasoned fishermen by surprise.

The fishermen's families had gathered on the shoreline waiting and waiting and praying for the safety of their men.

From a fleet of five small boats, only three had returned. Carlos's father was one of the missing.

After the mourning and burial, Carlos's mother had lost all interest in living. He, in turn, had postponed his career plans to help his mother raise the fatherless family. He took odd jobs, working at the local sisal plant, then apprenticed as a car mechanic at his uncle's shop making extra money for his personal use on the side with his clown act.

It had taken a long time for Carlos to tell his story. More than the one coffee session. In fact, it was on their third weekly coffee session when Carlos said, in halting English, "so you know about me *ahora*." He smiled.

Selene smiled back. Ever since they had shared coffee, she developed a soft spot for this sad Mexican clown who tugged at her heartstrings. Mike didn't mind their sessions together.

He told her only that she had better not give him any more pesos when they bumped into his clown act on a street corner. "He's taken them all with you buying him coffee," Mike half-teased. "We don't owe him anything."

But when Selene suggested they hire Carlos to help build their retreat and maybe manage the Yucatecan workers, Mike had abruptly refused.

Even when Selene pointed out it would be helping one of the locals get his life back on track. Mike would not reconsider.

Selene accused Mike of making decisions without her input. Maybe portraying a controlling side that irritated her. Perhaps a bit of jealousy over Carlos. Whatever, she didn't like the trait.

For her part, Selene knew she was taking more than a slight interest in Carlos. She had looked forward to these coffee meetings and missed them these past three months while she and Mike had been busy establishing their Retreat, arranging financing, looking after a thousand-and-one details.

She sensed Carlos felt the same way towards her, too. Each time they sat across from one other, Selene felt his dark eyes mentally undress her.

In turn, she tried hard not to touch him.

***

Now, on this perfect early morning welcomed by the warm sun, she lifted herself from the eco-pool in the newly completed eco-retreat, dancing along the natural path of grass.

She heard an unexpected male greeting.

"*Hola!*" came a familiar voice from the front office.

"Carlos!" she exclaimed. Her heart skipped a beat.

Chapter Ten

Drinking *Molson's* with Copley in *Mexicali Rose* --- the only bar in Brighton that carried *Patron Anejo*, Copley's favourite tequila --- Tommy began to unwind.

On his third round, he glanced around the seamy bar walls: splashes of faded red, green and white paint showed off mounted Mexican sombreros that invited bored customers to a more colourful world south of the U.S. border. In four hours, you could fly to Mexico from Toronto.

Copley was a world traveller: had lived one winter with his gay partner in Mérida, capital city of Mexico's Yucatán Peninsula. Admitted he loved the land and its people. Not sure why he was now stuck in small town Ontario running a fish 'n chips food truck with his partner.

Despising his cousin's personal lifestyle, Tommy still admired Copley's worldliness. In turn, he knew Copley looked up to him, idolized him like when they were kids. Yet for all his tough guy bravado, Tommy liked to bounce personal problems off his cousin. He knew Copley listened with fascination, as if in awe of Tommy and his powerful command of life.

"You and MJ having another problem?" Copley dipped his taco chip into the guacamole.

"Smart guy." Tommy playfully poked Copley's shoulder. "She's acting skitterish lately. Avoids me when we're in the house together."

"Fight a lot?"

"Naw. Not really. Afraid of me. Doesn't want me upset. So shuts up. Doesn't idolize me like you, Cop."

Cop smiled, nodded. "Sounds like a great relationship."

Tommy shrugged. "Better than the alternative."

"Which is...?" Copley sipped his *Patron*, looked sideways along the bar at his much bulkier cousin. The guacamole was beginning to brown.

"...the street."

Copley nodded. "So. Whatcha gonna do now? Or do you care?"

"'Course I care. Want her back the way she used to be." Which might mean physical restraint, he didn't add. Tommy still believed the best method of persuasion was brute force. Probably why he never made use of his degree. Opened a carpenter shop instead in town. Talented with his hands when he used them constructively rather than threatening Mary Jane or someone else.

After high school, where Tommy often physically defended the more genteel Copley, the cousins separated. Tommy headed off to university to study psychology. Copley wandered around Mexico and Central America, picked up Spanish along the way, before returning to work in the local fish and chips truck with his partner.

After Tommy's reappearance, Copley noticed his cousin seemed more dangerous. Dark events happened to the big man at university, Copley decided. He figured Tommy couldn't, wouldn't share those big city secrets with him. Not that he wanted to know. Tommy would have snapped at the slightest hint he was mentally unstable.

"How long you been with MJ now?" Cop peered over his dark-rimmed owl glasses, shoved his hair out of his eyes.

"Over 20 years."

"Long time, man. Lots of relationships run into trouble much sooner."

They had settled into a bar booth. Cop ordered another *patron*. Asked for fresh guacamole. And more taco chips.

"Always treated MJ like an honest to goodness husband even if we didn't marry. You know I took pity on her after her kid was taken away. Took her in. Treated her like a fragile doll. Knew she was delicate..."

Copley intervened, as if teasing, but not really. "Sure you weren't thinking about a slave relationship with a very pretty and yielding girl? Unwed. Ashamed. Guilty. Turned out by her family. What choice did she have?"

Tommy glared. Nodded. Sometimes Cop went right to the heart of the matter.

"So now what's the problem, man?"

Tommy cleared his throat. "Want to marry her now."

"What?" Cop was flabbergasted. "Why now? After all these years?"

"She's more interested in books and politics and philosophy than in my carpenter shop and hobby farming."

"…and you."

Tommy bit his tongue. Copley obviously knew his perceptive remark would upset him. You don't tell Tommy what he doesn't want to hear. Except maybe for Cop.

Then came Tommy's confession as he saw the situation. "MJ's worked at the library for years. She's become…" flailed his arms looking for the right word, "…distant. I blame that damn place."

"She favouring more independent ideas?" prompted Copley.

Tommy nodded. "So, I suggested we get married."

"Go on," said Copley, a bit surprised.

"About time, I said. Want to make you an honest woman, I said."

"And….?"

"Know what she said?"

Copley shook his head.

"No thank you, she said. I'm comfortable the way things are." Tommy's face turned beet red. "Can you believe that?!"

Copley shrugged. As if afraid to rattle Tommy's cage.

"W-e-l-l!" Tommy raised his voice. He watched the gentle Copley shrink. Liked to watch him cower every now and then. Increased his power image. "Called her an ungrateful little slut. Warned I could kick her out of my house this minute….!"

"What'd she say?"

"She said we could talk about it again another day! And then she turned her back on me to finish her coffee!"

Copley could only imagine the scene and Tommy's flaring temper.

"Told her I didn't like the tone of her voice…she didn't seem to care what I said! Know the worst thing, Copley?" Tommy shook his fist in the air.

"What?"

"You know I keep an eye on her…"

Copley nodded. Everyone in this small town knew that was no secret.

"Well," seethed Tommy through hissing teeth, "I suspect she's seeing someone. Can't stand the idea! When I find out who it is, I'll kill them both!" Stopped, thought, reworded his threat. "No. I'll kill him. But I'll keep her. Locked up."

Copley finished his guacamole in a hurry and drained his glass.

Chapter Eleven

By God, thought Alex, as he raced his white compact Ford back to his men's shop on Main Street after his hot chocolate at Timmy's, she *is* serious about this adventure. Leaving this town. Driving to Mexico. He knew he had to put pieces in place in a hurry. Some type of game plan. He knew she didn't have one. Only a strong desire to leave. Now.

OMG…this was the most exciting thing that had ever happened to him, he admitted. He had always loved MJ. Ever since Grade Six. And this running away idea appealed to his adventurous side that lay dormant for too many years. He had always been so boring, he thought. Never took chances. Well, now, he shivered in anticipation, just watch me, World!

He could hardly wait for the library to open tomorrow. He could think of nothing but her desire to get to Mexico. She was desperate to find her daughter. And she was desperate for his company and his help. It didn't matter that she expressed only a need to leave this town. There appeared no outward affection towards him, he admitted. But he didn't care about that right now.

Oh, how often he had wished he could have MJ for himself! They had been childhood lovers --

or so he thought -- until her pregnancy. That was so difficult to understand. Who could possibly have been the father? But he shook his head, that was a question for another day.

When he had been with her just now at Timmy's, he was prepared to offer his services to take her to Mexico. His heart jumped, his senses tingled, at the thought of the two of them driving together night and day to get to -- where was it? -- the Yucatán? He must look it up on a map!

When they parted at the coffee shop, Alex had locked his blue eyes with her green ones. He nodded, ever so slightly, a nod filled with meaning and desire and love. She nodded back, almost imperceptibly, but nevertheless, a nod. Then both had exited. Different doors. Two different cars. But on the same wavelength.

When Alex stormed into his store out of breath, he knew his store manager, Steve, must have wondered about the commotion. From the corner of his eye, he saw Steve raise an eyebrow at his boss's hurricane entrance as he carried on conversing with a late-night customer. Good, thought Alex! The less his manager knew, the better. He flew into his office, opened the safe, drew out some cash, credit cards, and his passport. Fortunately, he lived over the store in a small bachelor apartment. He tore up the stairs and began packing. Everything he needed he could stuff into two carry-ons.

Halfway through the evening, he realized he hadn't eaten. Opening the fridge door, he grabbed a couple of eggs. Scrambled eggs on toast were calling him to fill that gaping hole in his stomach.

After spending the rest of the night on the computer, plotting a route, researching the Yucatán, trying to calm his beating heart, rehearsing what to tell Steve and leaving instructions for his business, he nervously paced the floor.

He could barely sleep that night, his stomach in knots, his mind a whirling mess. But when his thoughts grilled down to the nitty gritty, his heart told him this was the adventure he had dreamed about for a long time with the woman he had always loved.

***

"Hi," he said with forced calm when he heard her voice over the library extension the next morning, "I'm packed now. So, I damn well hope you're serious about leaving!" It was his feeble attempt at a joke. God, he hoped it wasn't!

There was a chuckle, a hint of hysterical excitement on the other end. "I am. More than ever. Glenda connected with her Yucatecan library contact. And guess what? She replied immediately! Emailed saying she'd love to have an extra pair of hands to help an assistant she just hired for the Maya project. Listen to this…"

And she quickly read the online note from Glenda's friend Bonnie, Head of the Library for English Speakers (LES), in Mérida. MJ's eyes raced through it.

Hi Glenda! Long time no speak. Missing you even if we don't connect regularly.

Am certainly in need of some longterm help here. Need experienced reference librarian to help catalogue large collection of bequeathed papers from a Spanish mission house. Rare insights into early Maya life. Know any likely prospects? Would be forever grateful. Hope all's well with you.

Best, Bonnie.

P.S. for the right person there's a decent remuneration package.

MJ couldn't hide her excitement.

"Can you pick me up after work?" she asked.

Alex knew both of them were taking a terrible chance being seen together. His skin prickled. But MJ had also told him Tommy was about one hour away in Carleton Place, working on a woodworking project in a private home.

"What time?"

"5:30...have to get last minute instructions and information from Glenda. And then," she half-whispered, "please take me to your place until I decide how to handle the next few hours."

Alex gulped. Despite his bravado and the emotional high of helping MJ escape, getting his face rearranged by Tommy was not an option he relished.

***

"What did you tell your manager?" she asked when they were alone in his flat together.

"Don't worry. It's all taken care of. He knew I've been complaining about needing a holiday. Told him I got a last-minute flight…."

"But you didn't say to Mexico!..."

"Don't worry, MJ. He asked so I told him cuz it wouldn't help if I lied to him. Doesn't bother me…"

MJ looked distressed. "I still haven't worked out the details, Alex, but we don't need Tommy knowing where we're headed."

She found herself suddenly wrapped in his strong arms. "Shhhh. Don't worry…." he soothed.

"Alex…" She didn't get far.

They fell together on his sofa and at once, Alex found her mouth. Open. Wet. Longing. And she a willing partner.

Afterwards, he rolled his tongue around in her ear and whispered, "it'll be okay, MJ. You'll see."

She lay transfixed and then suddenly…

"Ohmygod, Alex, I've gotta go. Need to get home before he does." She straightened her dress, fixed her hair, applied fresh lipstick, shaking a little as they ran down the stairs from his apartment and to his car.

He gallantly held open the car door and she slid into the front seat. The only words she uttered on the way to Tommy's house were "hope he's not there or there will be hell to pay. Better let me out around the corner, Alex. I'll walk the rest of the way. And somehow, I'll call or connect with you."

Blew him a kiss as she sidled out of the car, looked around to see if there were any witnesses, straightened herself, turned to face the house, walked toward it without looking back.

Ohmygod, she thought as she saw Tommy's jeep in its familiar place in the garage, *he's home. I pray to God he hasn't seen anything...*

The trick was, she told herself, to act as normally as possible. She was late because she worked overtime. What depressed her was she was hoping to get home earlier to get her passport, some cash, put together some clothes…if only she hadn't dallied. But her dalliance with Alex had been delightful, she had to admit. Playful. Gentle. She knew Alex wasn't the man of her dreams but he could help her get to where she wanted: on the road to Mexico.

As soon as she opened the door, he was on her like a cat on a mouse.

"Where you been, MJ?" he demanded.

"Where d'you think?" She realized she was no longer terrified of Tommy, only mildly

frightened. She was learning how to handle him –
finally -- and she knew he was miffed after she
refused his long-awaited marriage proposal that she
had wanted forever. Now she didn't care.

"At that goddamn library!? All this time?
You're usually home way before this!"

She noticed he was studying her face. She
bit her lip, willing herself to behave nonchalantly.

"Where else? I told you I've been working
on a special project and I got caught up in it, that's
all. You get caught up in your projects. By the way,
how's the one you're doing now?"

He glared at her. "Don't change the
subject!" he yelled.

Once upon a time, Tommy's ranting and
raving upset her. But lately, no. And now, definitely
not.

"You mean, you can change the subject. But
I can't?" she shot back hotly.

"What is this, lady?!" Stepping forward, he
grabbed her wrist, began twisting it. MJ turned,
leaned to follow the hold, lessening its pressure.
Tommy suddenly released it.

"Look MJ," he breathed. "I'm tired of this
bickering. Let's start again. Why are you late?"

Now MJ knew he was softening. The
stronger she was, the more he backed off. It took
her years to reach this plateau. But she still couldn't
read his brain. He was moving closer to her. A look
of disbelief? Fury? What?

He began to sniff. Like a dog. Sniffed her hair. Her clothes.

"You goddam little slut," he said in a quiet, violent tone. "I smell a man. Who the hell you bin fucking? I know sure as hell it ain't me!" he snarled. Caught her off guard. Knocked her down. Began kicking.

MJ curled into the fetal position to protect herself from his blows.

Chapter Twelve

At the sound of his voice, Selene's heart skipped a beat. She ran to the Retreat's office. And there, in all his dark-haired, dark-skinned glory, stood Carlos. His smile overwhelmed her. How much she had missed him…

She melted into his open arms. Loved his After Shave lotion smell. Momentarily mused, *why do all Latino men use some kind of after-shave?*

"Carlos!" she whispered, snuggling into him. "I did not expect to see you again."

"Why not?" he asked, in perfect English.

"Wow… listen to your English!"

"Yes. After you disappeared into this…" he paused, "…*proyecto* of yours and Mike, I decided I'd better learn English. For me. For my future. But especially for you." He hugged her while Selene's face turned upwards and smothered him with kisses.

He stepped back to admire her. "I miss you."

"Oh, Carlos, I didn't realize how much I missed you, too, until suddenly you turn up in front of me! Mike is not here right now…" she playfully ignored the roll of his eyes. She touched his hand. "Let me take you on a short tour of what we've accomplished so far."

Holding his hand, she led him through the office to the Retreat's interior. His mouth opened wide when he saw the aqua blue pool before him.

"Wow! *Mucho* impressed!"

"Yes. It's beautiful, isn't it? I just took a swim. Want to jump in?"

"Wearing what?" teased Carlos. "I didn't bring a --- how do you say *traje de baño*? --- a bathing suit."

"You don't need one right now," she smiled. "No-one else is around."

"Except you." He quickly removed his jeans and slung them nonchalantly over a nearby tree trunk.

Selene could only stare. "You are absolutely beautiful," she finally breathed.

Without effort, he dove into the pristine waters. He was underwater so long, Selene feared he had bumped his head. But she could see his lithe body halfway to the other side. He finally emerged, sputtering, laughing, at the far end.

"My God," she muttered to herself. "you are gorgeous." Aloud she called, "Didn't know you could hold your breath that long."

Carlos laughed. A genuinely deep throated chuckle that projected honest enjoyment. "Hand me that towel *por favor*!"

She almost shyly brought a towel and his jeans to his nakedness. He was aroused. Selene breathed slowly as she noticed his erection and slowly handed over his request. "My God," she said, aloud this time. "you *are* gorgeous!"

Slowly he hoisted up his jeans -- no underwear in sight -- and trying hard to conceal his erection, difficult as it was, he zipped up.

Selene played coy. She stared at his bulge and gulped. "That was some magic trick!" she exploded with longing.

He reached for her. His lips found hers. And their passion jumped back and forth until he whispered into her ear. "This is not the time or place, M," he breathed. "Let's look around. Show me yours -- and Mike's -- hard work."

She gulped. "Y-y-yes. You're right, Carlos." She sidled into his damp chest. Ran her fingers through his wet thick black hair. Her forefinger traced the shape of his straight nose to his generous mouth before he snatched it between his lips.

"Let me give you a quick tour," she shivered, "before you devour me!"

Her hand locked in his, Selene led Carlos to one of six unique cabañas surrounding the eco-pool. Each cabaña has a name, she explained. The one in front of them was called Ixtabay. "*Ish-ta-buy* is how we pronounce it," she said.

Carlos grinned. "You forget I am Maya and know this story well."

She looked into his dark warm eyes, smiled, looked down and shrugged. "Of course. What's your version?" she asked.

He grabbed her playfully by her long ponytail and then tucked it under his chin as he spoke. "An ancient Maya legend warns young men out walking alone at night of an enchanting spirit that takes the form of a beautiful woman and lures them to their death. The name of this spirit is Ish-ta-buy." He let go of her hair. "Am I right?"

She nodded with a smile.

"Why would you call a cabin used for sleeping a name like this?"

"Well, one of our carpenters stayed in that room and he swore he saw a vision of a woman dressed in black with long black hair. We actually had to get a shaman here to perform a purification ceremony. After that, no problem."

Carlos teased. "You have long black/reddish hair. Did you creep into his room at night?"

"No," she grinned. "But if it had been you, I might've!"

Selene could not get over the fact that Carlos, who had been out of sight but not out of mind while she and Mike built this place, was like a new person. He oozed confidence. He no longer slouched. No more furtive eyes. He stared at her, melting her resolve not to become involved with him. She had enough to deal with Mike.

"What's happened to you?" she teased seriously. "You're no longer a sad clown. You speak English. You are confident. Wha…at happened?"

"Got a good paying job as a mechanic. Took English lessons with Daveed. You 'member heem?

We spent many hours, heem and me, jus practisin',
practisin', practisin'…"

She smiled. Squeezed his hand.

"We offer a place to relax in a balanced eco
system," she continued with her spiel. "Nutritious
meals with fruits and vegetables grown in the Maya
village near us. It's been a dream of mine to meld
the old with the new. Introduce culturally starved
tourists with the ancient wise ways of the Maya."

"So, how's it going?" They had circled the
enclave and were back at the beginning.

"Not bad. We're not fully open yet but the
tourist bureau reps have been here. Even the *Diario*
wrote a piece about us, took some photos. I've
spoken with some Maya ladies in the village. They
seem keen to share our dream. We'll pay them of
course. Teach the curious how to make their own
corn tortillas the traditional way. Or visit those who
weave those colourful hammocks outside their
Maya homes. Or perhaps be spiritually purified by
a Maya healer who uses herbs, intonations and
incense to cleanse our inner selves…."

She glanced quickly at Carlos. "Are you
listening to a word I said?"

"Absolutely. I'm -- how do you say it? --
fascinated. I especially like watching you talk."

Selene jabbed him playfully in his ribs. "Tell
me what's been happening with you now. Aside
from the super job and the fact we can communicate
now. You need to teach me Spanish!"

"Well, things have changed a bit at *mi casa*. My uncle -- my father's brother, *el hermano de mi padre* -- has suddenly appeared. Supposedly to help our *familia*... "

"Wonderful!" exclaimed Selene.

Only...." and Carlos paused.

"Only what?"

"Well, he used to be a priest. But no more. That's really why he's here with us now."

"What do you mean, Carlos. Used to be…a priest?"

"Well, he won't talk to me about it but mom said the Church kicked him out."

Selene's eyes shot open. "What? That's serious stuff, Carlos."

"*Si,* guess he was sexually abusing young girls for many years. Finally, the Church let him go. So, we're not pleased he's with us. My mom hopes he gets a decent job and helps with money. He speaks English very well. He actually served in Canada."

But just as Selene was about to comment about his uncle having been a cleric in Canada, they both heard loud scraping sounds as the front door to the Retreat opened with a clang.

In strode Mike. Frowned. Looked at Carlos. Then Selene. "So what's going on?" he asked snarkly. To Carlos he threw out, "and what's the clown doing here?"

Chapter Thirteen

The front door bell rang.

Tommy cursed under his breath. Stopped berating MJ who lay curled on the floor in fear, immobile. "Get up!" he ordered. "Go to the bedroom! I'll see to you later!"

MJ bolted to the bedroom. She didn't know who was at the door, didn't care, but it gave her the opening she needed. Wanted. Once upon a time, like a little slave, she'd do exactly what Tommy ordered and stay put, meekly accepting whatever punishment he dealt. But not now. Not ever again!

She raced to their bedroom, grabbed her private papers, portfolio, passport. Quietly, swiftly closed the bedroom door. She could still hear Tommy being his usual fake over-the-top friendly self in the background as she stealthily crept to the back porch, fiddled at the damn latch---*oh please open*---closed it silently, then dashed, flew around the side of the house now in the last throes of twilight, away from the front door towards Harry's house next door. His yard connected with the road where Alex had left her not that long ago.

Oh, gawd! Harry's damn dog. Barking. "Shhhh!" she commanded. Kept running. Scratched herself through Harry's hemlock hedge. Hit the road. Kept to the ditch on the side. Ran. And ran.

Dodged any headlights from passing cars. Thank God it was twilight now!

Knew immediately where she was headed. Alex's place. Her only safe haven.

Dammit! She'd been seen! The car that just passed was backing up. Quickly MJ sprinted across the road. Hid in a cedar clump on the other side. Who was in that car! Wasn't Tommy but who? Oh gawd, now biting bugs were driving her crazy!

The car stopped opposite. She strained her ears. Actually, she thought, the white car looked familiar. Then she heard a voice calling softly, almost hysterically, from the driver's window: "MJ!" Pause. "MJ!" Urgently.

Alex!

Tore through the bushy hedge. Reached the passenger side. Ripped open the unlocked door. Jumped inside. Slammed shut the door. Slid to the floor.

Immediately there was a gasp from Alex who only now realized she was his passenger.

"MJ!" he blurted.

"Drive, Alex," she ordered breathlessly. "….to your place. We've got to leave as soon as possible!"

"MJ…."

"Don't talk… catch up later.."

***

Tommy was beyond annoyed. That was some dumb conversation at the door. Some stupid ass hoping Tommy might want to hire him in his business. Heard around town he had his own carpentry shop. This idiot claiming he was really good at his job and he'd like to help Tommy make more money. And some for himself, of course. Chuckle. Chuckle. Went on about how he knew about different kinds of wood for different jobs and yada yada yada….

Down the hall he marched. Threw open the bedroom door to a dark room.

"MJ!" Tommy flipped on the lights impatiently. "Okay, doll, we playing a game now? I love games. You know that." He opened the closet door. Swooshed his hand through her clothes expecting to hit her. Nothing. Scanned the bottom of the closet where she was probably cowering in fear.

Nothing. Surely not under the bed like a child? Lifted the comforter. Peered under the bed. "MJ?" "MJ!" Now angry. Bumped around the room. Pulled out the ottoman. Pulled open the curtains. Where the hell could she be?

Out in the hall, he took the stairs, two at a time, to the second floor. Ripped into the office. "MJ?" Looked around quickly. Ripped into the second bedroom…then into the bathroom… "MJ?" All the while he was thinking he'd ram his fist down her throat when he caught her. She couldn't make a fool out of him like this. He'd mess up her face a little so she couldn't go to work. Fuck her hard. Where was that pussy of his?

Finally, the thought struck, she may have left the house. Couldn't believe that possible. But how? Thundered back down the stairs. Through the kitchen. Saw the latch on the screen door on the back porch. She leave this way? Had to, he thought. Couldn't use the front door. Couldn't get out the latched windows with secured screens.

Bellowed: "MJ, if you are in this house you'd better come out right now! Or you won't recognize yourself in the mirror! This is no longer a game!"

Added: "Your last chance, doll!"

Silence.

At once he tore out the front door. His jeep was still there. Ran next door. Had no idea how dishevelled and distraught he looked.

"No, haven't seen her! Why would I?" Harry firmly closed the door in Tommy's angry red face.

Tommy tore down the road. Running as fast as he could. No sign of MJ. No sign of anything. He raged like a caged wild beast.

Chapter Fourteen

Mike's harsh greeting stunned Carlos. And Selene.

Embarrassed, she tried to smooth out the rudeness of Mike's remarks. "So, you didn't have a good run this morning?" she joked. But it wasn't working. She felt Carlos freeze beside her. "I should go," he muttered in perfect English. "See you guys later." And he strode out of the office, slamming the door behind him.

Selene turned on Mike. "What in God's name is your problem?! Why were you so rude to him? He only came to see how we were doing…."

"Uh, uh, babe," snarled Mike. "He came to see you. I'm a man. And I know the ways of men like him. He wants to fuck you big-time."

Selene bit her tongue. What if Mike knew *she* wanted to fuck Carlos?

Instead, she threw out, "well, thanks for the vote of confidence, Mikey-boy! Guess what? Since we're not exactly on talking terms, I've decided to take the bus into Mérida this morning. Think I'll work for awhile with Bonnie at the LES. And then maybe stay for their feature presentation on Frida Kahlo. I'll certainly feel more welcome there than here."

Running fingers through her ponytail, she turned to leave the office. Mike reached for her, grabbed her arm. "Listen, Selene, I've had lots of people tell me how you and Carlos sat with goo goo eyes at each other while you two drank coffee. Lots of coffee dates. He'd love to have a piece of your ass. And I just don't feel like letting him do that."

"I don't belong to you, Mike. Just because we're business partners doesn't mean I'm tied to you!" She flung his hand aside and fled out the office door to her room.

On the bus ride into Mérida, she tried to forget Mike and his jealousy and her growing attraction to Carlos, concentrating instead on her last conversation with Bonnie. Untidy conversations like the one with Mike upset her. And then she'd lapse into anxiety or insecurity. Which used to lead to alcohol. So she forced herself to think about Bonnie and the LES.

A fellow Canadian, Bonnie initially arrived in Progreso to teach English, moved 30 minutes away to the state capital of Mérida, and was now head librarian at LES.

The Library was a sort of community activity and arts beacon for the many English-speaking expats who now made the Yucatán their home.

During one of many interactive sessions with Bonnie, Selene had explained how the Maya had captured her imagination. That led to Bonnie mentioning her librarian friend, coincidentally from the same area in Ontario where Selene once lived. Through her, Bonnie had connected with a MaryJane, a woman whose interest in the Maya was almost off the charts. "This woman" almost insisted she get a chance to work on any Maya research in their homeland.

"Like, why look a gifthorse in the mouth? So, she's on her way to Mérida now, driving all the way from Canada. She lives in Brighton, not far from Ottawa where you're from so maybe you two might hit it off. Except she's old enough to be your mother."

"When she's expected?" Selene had asked.

"Any day now 'til I heard about the flooding around Villahermosa in Tabasco. Bet she's tied up there, waiting it out. Can you imagine driving all the way from Canada?"

Selene didn't bother going into detail how she and Mike had motorbiked from Canada, through the U.S., and then down the Mexican east coast to Mérida and finally, to Progreso. Not many people make that run but more than a handful judging by the Canadian license plates on the odd car in Progreso and Mérida, she mused. Then their own car, not a rental, was at their disposal.

"Anyway, I'm introducing you two when she gets here," chattered on Bonnie. "I'm hoping you'll enjoy researching the Maya world together. My goal for you both is to set up a reputable Maya historic library so we can go to the city fathers and hopefully get a grant to continue our work." Bonnie paused.

Selene could tell Bonnie's mind was whirling with her next idea.

"Then, when she goes back, maybe you could tag along." Bonnie paused, as if not sure what to say or where to go from here. "It's one way out of a bad situation here, Selene. Frankly, I'm worried about you sliding backwards. You've got a lot of talent but you'll just drown if you hang around here too long with boozing expats."

Her comment rankled Selene. She resented that last remark and simmered for a minute before she spoke. "You forget our eco-retreat," she retorted. "Anyone who's a loser wouldn't even consider starting a project like ours. It's looking better and better now that we've got the finished *palapas* around the pool. I've even chatted with some of the village women who seem to be okay -- in fact even enthusiastic – about helping tourists how to cook, how to weave…even the *Diario* wrote a piece about us. Came and took photos. Gave us what we need at this point. Publicity. Already we're getting calls from tourist companies asking if we will accept reservations. We're not quite that ready yet. Although, we're close."

Bonnie acquiesced with a smile. "Maybe I was a little too hasty in my judgement, Selene. I hope everything goes super well. It's only because

I've seen far too many expats become bored and reach for the bottle during my time here. I'm hopeful you and this woman will hit it off together."

Selene half smiled. *I hope Bonnie is right,* she thought…*she and this Canadian librarian friend of hers might be able to work together well to study an ancient civilization. Keep each other encouraged and grounded.*

Now, on this returning bus ride to Progreso, Selene's busy mind continued on overdrive.

Despite the easy breezy reply she blew off after Bonnie referenced her flighty reputation, Selene still felt a fluttering uneasiness.

Selene's mind raced back to her last conversation with Mike. Maybe he was right. She was always flitting this way and that. Never quite settled.

For example, Selene thought, she *was* very attracted to Carlos now. And it was obvious Carlos felt the same way about her.

This time, with a new business beginning and maybe a new man, Selene had no time or energy to waste on booze. *Wait girl,* she chastised, *you're getting way ahead of yourself!*

Even in her strongest moments, Selene wondered whether she could pull off a successful business and enjoy a strong personal relationship with a new man at the same time.

Chapter Fifteen

Only when they were back safely in Alex's apartment did MJ break her code of silence.

"The guy's a madman, Alex! For all I know he might have killed me tonight if you hadn't come to the door. I've got to leave immediately. Get out of here. Are you still willing to drive to Mexico? Were you serious when you agreed?"

She flashed her emerald green eyes at him, staring into his soul. She knew their past lovemaking had tipped the scales in her favour. Maybe she wasn't nuts over Alex, but he was a gentle lover. And a good one at that. Maybe she'd really fall for him later, given the chance.

"Look," she flaunted her purse and waved her passport in front of his eyes. "I'm ready! I know I don't have any clothes but I can buy some along the way. There's no way I'm going back to that house, Alex. He's probably lying in wait. And God knows what strings he'll pull to start a search for me right here in Brighton! He may have started already…most of the cops are in his pocket…he has something on everyone!"

"I meant every word I said to you, MJ. Leave now or wait 'til morning?" Alex stared at her.

"It'll be a wild ride."

"And that's exactly what I want," came his quick reply.

"Will he know it's you I'm going with?"

Alex shrugged. "Can't see how. Not sure he'd be able to pick me out of a police line-up. He seemed so distracted when I was at your door. Humouring me almost. Wanted me to get the hell out of there."

"Yes. Yes. I heard him at the door. For sure, he wanted to get back to kicking me."

Alex winced.

She realized Alex had risked his own safety to protect her.

Suddenly, there was a banging downstairs at his door. She looked at Alex who was frowning. "You expecting anyone?"

"No."

"Want to ignore it?"

"Better not. You know this town. Someone's sure to have heard the banging, will peek out behind closed curtains. No need to attract any attention."

"Quick," hissed MJ. "Give me a weapon…anything…frying pan, something to hit with…scare someone with…just in case…" She glanced quickly around his living room. Saw the fireplace poker in front of his fake fireplace. Grabbed it. To her surprise, the poker was not fake. It was iron. Heavy and secure in her hand.

Alex nodded swiftly. "An heirloom from my grandparents."

Banging at the door continued.

"All right, all right, just a minute, I'm coming," yelled Alex down the stairs. Before descending, he pointed to another door in the hall. "That leads down to the store," he whispered. "Just in case. You can get out the back door. Haven't bolted it yet." Pause. "Grab your purse and passport. Take it with you."

MJ heard Alex clump down the stairs. Open the door. Her heart stopped when she heard the voice.

"Howdy." It was Tommy! MJ's emerald eyes flashed with fear. Ears tuned into picking up minute sounds. Breath hanging on every overheard word.

"Er… oh, hi! What a surprise! Thought you'd dismissed me as a possible partner." MJ was in awe of Alex's cool-as-a-cucumber response. "What're you doing here now? Offering me a position?"

"Naw," said Tommy, almost amiably. MJ's reflexes hung on high alert.

"A neighbour happened to see you -- or at least I'm assuming it was you or your car by the sounds of the description -- pick up a woman on the road near my place," said Tommy suspiciously. "And I'm here to ask you about her."

Long pause.

"So, I'm assuming from your reaction you did pick her up. Zat so?" A ring of uncoiled anger laced his words.

As she crept towards the hall door that led downstairs to the store, MJ could tell Alex was stalling. The last words she heard were…

"How the hell you find out where I live?"

Twice in one night, MJ was on the run. Breathing in short gasps, she opened and quietly closed the clothing store's back door. Was about to flee down the back alley when she felt the poker in her hand. Solid. Heavy. Ready. Threw her purse and passport on a back picnic table. Began to circle to the front.

She could see him. Tommy standing defiantly at the door in front of Alex. Gradually she crept up behind him. God only knows when he would grab Alex and beat his face!

She had made the right decision. She could see Tommy grab Alex by his collar, threatening him with a clenched fist.

Slowly, silently, she knew the element of surprise was in her favour.

She was almost behind Tommy now, heard his threats, saw his ready fists…

Timing was everything she knew.

Raised the poker.

Alex must have looked beyond Tommy. Tommy turned.

And in that instant, MJ brought the poker down as hard as she could on Tommy's head.

Chapter Sixteen

When Selene stepped off the bus in Progreso, she did not walk straight back to their eco-retreat outside of town. Her inner voice had been chattering away during the 30-minute ride and she needed some downtime to calm herself.

So, she hung around the main square meandering towards the beach, thinking about her future. She thought she had it figured out with Mike. Although they weren't married, everyone considered them a 'couple'. But did she? Arguing with herself, she realized Mike was familiar, almost a brother, and sometimes they had hot sex but not as often as before. Worse, she didn't really care anymore. She was just as happy to drift off to sleep on her own.

True, they were business partners, pooling their savings to make this real estate deal happen for the eco-retreat. They both recognized their need to ground themselves somewhere and why not in this community of local fishermen and expats? They felt comfortably accepted.

Also true, this was a poor town, little more than a sleepy little fishing village on the shores of the Gulf of Mexico. The one main street led to Progreso's pier, a cement structure of 4 miles (6.5 km) long that reached out into the Gulf. The pier -- reputed to be the longest in the world – attracted investors with plans to extend it and capture the cruise ship trade. Sandy beaches on either side of the pier were also a drawing card for expats and tourists. She could almost imagine a Coney Park with the right investors.

As Selene lazily ambled along Calle 80, she began to fight her 'monkey' mind. She hated when she wandered all over the map in this mental state. Sauntering along the *malecon* in front of the beach, she approached her nemesis, *Amigos*. Almost near the bar's entrance, she stopped. No, she told herself, I will NOT go into that bar. Even though she and Mike had worked there on-and-off for Pedro, the owner. Even though she knew Pedro would welcome her with open arms.

But unseen forces played with her busy mind. Before she knew it, she was inside.

Amigos faces the Gulf and has a movie set appearance with swaying rattan lampshades covering solitary lightbulbs and a thatched roof. On entering and squinting through the dimly lit interior, Selene caught sight of a table of expats she wanted desperately to avoid. So, she sat alone at the bar, ordered a *Dos Equis cerveza*, her first sip of alcohol in months.

As she rolled the once familiar tasting liquid around in her mouth, she thought strangely enough, about her parents. On FaceTime last week, they practically begged her to come home for a visit. Her father really wasn't well these days, heart problems, said her mother tearfully. "You've been gone for four years now without a visit home," her mother painfully reminded her. Although, Selene reminded her, she'd kept in touch, as regular as clockwork, almost bi-weekly. Money, she knew, wasn't a problem. Her wealthy parents would forward travel funds immediately.

She quickly decided her parents had no reason to know she was a recovering alcoholic. She snorted as she raised the beer bottle to her mouth. Her parents. Again, her monkey mind began to play. Her worst memory flooded back to her.

She sipped her beer.

She did remember once, she recalled, when she was in grade six, there was a mousy little girl who whispered to her in the playground: *'did you know you were adopted?'*.

Selene looked at her and froze. What was this idiot girl saying? All Selene knew was that she never forgot that ugly whisper. She remembers tearing home after school, impatiently waiting for her mom to come home from work, biting her nails, frantically charging all over the house, until finally she heard the back door open and close.

"Am I adopted?" she had demanded in tears.

Her mother dropped her briefcase at once.

"What?"

"Am I adopted?" she had screamed at her mother. "Joanne at school says I'm adopted! I want to know! Am I adopted!?"

She remembered how she couldn't read her mother's face. As if a mask had immediately fallen across her face.

In fact, Selene had noticed her mother's voice become unusually calm when she replied: "what do YOU think, Selene? Do you think your father and I don't love you with all our hearts? Do you not know there is nothing we wouldn't do for you?"

Selene wasn't sure why but her mother's defiant answer did not quell her doubts. And then, later, after dinner, she knew her gut instinct had been right.

"It's time we talked," said her father. "You need to understand a few things...."

Added her mother. "We've been waiting for the right time." Selene's heart raced. She watched her mother fidget. She watched her father stare strangely into space. Almost as if he was there physically but not mentally.

And then came the story of her adoption. It almost blew her away. *Almost.*

Because at times, when things weren't going well in her life, she had studied her parents. An underlying, niggling germ suggested another scenario. Did she look like either of them? Hard to tell. To her, her skin looked darker; certainly, her hair was this black-reddish colour. Her mother was a bottle blonde, though. Had always dyed her hair. And her father didn't have any.

She was beyond astonished with what she heard: her mother, an unwed 16-year-old from Brighton, a town about an hour from Ottawa; her father unknown.

Her father spoke now. "Because we knew the girl's background…she was a good girl we understand but unfortunately got pregnant and…." her father's shoulders shrugged. "We thought we could offer you a stable home with a solid upbringing so you could have a better future."

Despite her anger, Selene softened a little. "Do you know anything about her?"

"Your mother? Definitely a good-looking young woman, auburn or russet-coloured hair…." Selene immediately touched her head, "and beautiful emerald green eyes." Selene flashed her blue-green eyes. "I went in to see her myself. Not to tell her we were adopting you but just to get a feel for her as a human being. You know?" Her adoptive mother stopped.

Her father suddenly looked tired. Selene was hanging on his every word. "She was a fine young woman, Selene. Scared. Crying. Upset…."

"She didn't want to give me up?"

"I don't think she knew what was happening. She only knew she couldn't keep you…"

"…and so, she was crying…?"

"Yes. Crying. A lot. Sobbing."

Selene's imagination immediately took her to her young mother's side. She thought she could taste her anguish.

"What about my father?"

"We don't know," her father shrugged. "We don't know anything about the man who was your father. She left that part of the hospital documentation blank…not an uncommon thing to do under those circumstances at the time…"

"Where was this?"

Her father's furrow deepened. He sighed. "In the Ottawa Valley."

"Where?"

"Does it matter?"

"To me. Yes. It does."

"In Brighton. An hour away from Ottawa."

"Did she give you anything for me? A note? Piece of jewellery? Anything?"

"Your name. Maya. Which we changed."

Selene looked at them both. "My middle name is Maya."

They nodded. "We felt we should honour her request since she was your birth mother." Selene felt a whisper of gratitude towards her adoptive parents.

"Why didn't you tell me sooner?"

"We kept meaning to, really we did, Selene. But this is a difficult conversation and every time we thought we could, we couldn't." It was her father who spoke.

"What we didn't want to happen, has happened," said her mother, tearfully. "You found out from someone else. No wonder you are angry. No wonder you aren't eating. We are so sorry, Selene. We had no idea this was going to happen."

Humbled, at once physically ill, Selene's emotions were ragged.

She watched her adoptive parents cringe as she pummelled them with questions. She was being cruel. But she had to know everything she could.

After a major emotional meltdown, Selene had stopped dwelling on her adoption. But never her birth mother. She had charged ahead with life, although always aware of that dull ache in her heart.

Try as she did, she could never trace her birth mother. She immediately searched using available online services: *adopted.com, Adoption Council of Ontario, Quora, Facebook...*

No matter, she was not successful. She believed in time that she would find her. But then, what would she say? Would her mother ever want to see her again? For years, Selene's search drove her crazy.

In fact, her union with Mike had begun as a welcome adventure. A new beginning. Both in their second year at Ottawa's Carleton University, Mike, studying commerce, and Selene in psychology, each had decided independently to chuck life in the *same-old* lane and take off on his motorbike to Mexico. Her parents had been horrified; Mike's parents, from smalltown Ontario, were not.

So now, after a few misadventures here and there, she was in this little town of Progreso, in a bar, determined to take control of her life. She and Mike were carving out a small business and Selene was sure she was on her feet again. Whether she and Mike stayed together was not the point. In fact, she didn't seem to mind they might be business partners with separate private lives.

Bored – and trying to squash her hyperactive monkey mind -- she looked above the bar into the wall-to-wall mirror. Her eyes roamed over the dark interior via the mirror. She saw the expats, getting louder and louder and ruder near the entrance. Over in one corner, she spied Pedro, the bar owner, with his newest daughter in his arms, at a table of regular patrons. Her eyes cased the rest of the bar. There was some guy in the darkest corner chatting earnestly but quietly to a very pretty young woman. Selene's eyes glanced back over the guy again. Although his back was facing her, he looked familiar. She began to study him. His girl partner looked enamoured. Excited. Her hands crossed the table as she tried to lock her fingers into his. Then he turned slightly and Selene caught his profile.

Carlos!

She couldn't help herself. Immediately, she slipped off the bar stool, beer bottle in hand, and with beating heart, deliberately sauntered over to the dark corner table.

Chapter Seventeen

"Oh my God…look at all the blood! Alex…what have I done?" Horrified, MJ stood over the still body of her tormentor Tommy as he lay slumped on the ground. Dark wet stains blanketed the concrete in front of the store. "His head is bleeding! Help! What should I do?"

Alex instantly grounded her. Grabbed her by her wrists.

"We get out of here right now," he said quietly, forcefully. "I'll call 911 on the way out of town. And we'll figure it out as we go."

In shock, MJ wailed. "I killed him!"

"He was going to kill you."

MJ stared at him in shock.

"You saved my life," said Alex. "He would've killed me. Now let's get moving. Like we planned. I'll call for help after we've left. Now get in the car!"

Speechless, MJ dumbly followed Alex's orders.

With one last backward glance at Tommy's crumpled body lying in blood from his head wound, a frowning MJ automatically picked up the poker -- she knew this could be incriminating evidence -- and carefully placed it on the floor in the back of the car. Quickly jumped into the front seat beside Alex. Buried her head in her hands in shock.

Alex calmly backed his white compact off the cement apron. Driving quickly, he pulled over after a couple of streets. The first call he made was to Steve, his manager. "Don't worry about Tommy," he said to a shaking MJ.

"Steve? Alex here. Listen, need your help. I know this is last minute but I have to leave town for a few days. You saw me belting up the stairs last night. Am in the middle of a hot deal. So, need you to take over management of the store. If you need help, I trust you to hire well. Yes," in reply to a question, "I'll be in touch with you. If anyone asks, just say I've had a personal matter I need to tend to..."

He stopped talking. Looked at the quiet street before him.

"Yeah, perfect," he continued, "thanks so much."

"And Steve, one more thing," Alex glanced at the white-faced MJ who was staring open-mouthed at him. "Am about to call 911. There's a guy bleeding on the concrete near the side of the store. He attacked me first. So, there will be lots of questions. Cover for me, pal, okay? Cuz you know nothing about this anyway. I owe you one. Thanks...." Alex hung up.

Then he dialled 911. "Need an emergency vehicle sent immediately to Alex's Men Shop on Brant. There's a man bleeding outside the store. Thanks." He quickly hung up.

"They can trace that call," whispered MJ. "They'll come looking…"

"In that case, MJ, guess we'd better move it," And he pointed the car towards the highway and headed for the Canadian/US border.

Still wordless, MJ's mind began to churn. In her head and heart, she knew they were doing the only thing they could right now. Getting out of town. Put as much distance between themselves and Tommy. OMG, Tommy! She thought back again to his lifeless body lying on the cement. Was it possible she had killed him?! Two strong emotions enveloped her.

The first was hate…she hated him! She hated how he had used her, abused her, pretended to 'protect' her, all the while holding her prisoner. She had no power, no-one to help her, until that lucky day he agreed to 'let' her work at the library! And that was only because she agreed to his sexual demands. That was the deal. She was his baby doll. He could rape her. Stick all manner of sex toys in her vagina, even food: cucumbers, a carrot, a banana that broke off, and once, shrimp! He said he wanted to know if they smelled the same as her crotch. She hated his blindfold game, couldn't tell where he was, how he would prod her, whether he wanted her to take him by mouth or anally.

The second was fear. Tommy was capable of killing people. In fact, she was pretty sure he had badly beaten some poor old woman who had complained to the Better Business Bureau about a woodworking project he had finished in her home but she didn't like it. MJ never forgot how he bragged about it, partially, she thinks, to frighten her. And it worked. "I took a solid piece of wood, one shaped like a bat and beat her around the head," he said matter-of-factly.

Despite suffering in a home prison against her will, MJ still felt she held the upper hand. In her mind and gut, she carried her strongest weapon. Her baby hole. Her daughter. Come hell or high water, Tommy or no Tommy, she was going to find her daughter. No matter what.

Meanwhile, she noticed Alex glance over at her, silently sitting beside him in his car as they drove through town to the highway.

As if from afar, she heard Alex's comforting voice.

"MJ," he said gently. "We're on our way."

Chapter Eighteen

Approaching his table, Selene gently placed her hand on his shoulder.

"Carlos?" she said softly. Immediately, Selene noticed the girl's hand swiftly withdraw from him.

Carlos wheeled around with surprise. He stood up.

"Selene!" he exclaimed, quickly taking her face in his hands, kissing her on each cheek a little too briskly. "What are you doing here, my friend? And with a beer in your hand?"

"Friend?" and Selene cocked her head. She felt a jealous streak run through her body as she acknowledged the young woman at his table. "Hi," she addressed the dark-haired beauty who was looking as surprised as Selene felt. "My name's Selene" and she held out her hand in greeting.

"Here. Come. Sit with us," said Carlos, pulling a chair over from a nearby empty table.

Selene could feel uneasy vibes from both Carlos and the young woman. "This is Rosalie," he said, as the three sat in an awkward silence.

"Am I interrupting something?" asked Selene.

She caught Carlos and Rosalie quickly exchanging knowing glances. Carlos looked more squeamish than Rosalie, sensed Selene.

"We were just talking about our uncle," said Carlos.

"Uncle?" frowned Selene.

"Yes, the one I told you about who was kicked out of the Church in Canada. I told you how he left to live here with my family. We are having problems with this." To Rosalie, he spoke Spanish, *"Está bien hablar con Selene aquí. Somos buenos amigos."* "it's okay to talk with Selene here. We are good friends."

Selene didn't like the 'good friends' reference but let it pass since she felt a sudden surge of relief that Rosalie was not competing for Carlos's romantic affections. Suddenly Rosalie, the attractive 'cousin', was no threat.

In fact, she offered to butt out. "Sorry, I didn't mean to interrupt a family discussion. I just wasn't sure it was you, Carlos, so I had to come over and see." She smiled at Rosalie.

"Oh, it's okay, really," replied Carlos, looking at Rosalie. "Maybe another person's opinion outside the family might help. Rosalie has been living in Canada. She came back with my uncle and has been bringing me up to speed on his awful behaviour. It does not look good for our family. We are discussing where to go from here."

"Well, Carlos, the last time we were talking," and she looked at Rosalie while addressing Carlos, "you said he was sexually abusing women in his parish. Is that true, Rosalie?"

"*Si*..yes," said Rosalie, speaking for the first time. Her voice was soft and fluid, like her body, thought Selene. She was very attractive. Not for the first time, Selene found it difficult to understand why many Mexican women gained so much weight as they aged. Rosalie was a beauty now. But would she always be? Selene believed a steady diet of cola and sugar destroyed their health and good looks years ahead of their time. Right now, Rosalie was a beauty, in the prime of life.

At the same time, she was impressed by Carlos's English skills. "How did your English get so good so quickly?"

"I have been speaking nothing but English since Rosalie has returned. It's good for me but also makes it difficult for my family to understand what we're saying."

Carlos continued. "My mother is not pleased that Martin Garcia is back and living with our family. We are all working hard to make a decent living. As you know, Selene." He nodded her way.

"What can our uncle do to help us?" he continued. "Not much. He is not used to manual labour. He has always been looked after by the Church. And so, he is useless outside of it. My father was a proud man and I'm not sure he would have approved his brother coming back in disgrace.

I feel as the eldest of my four brothers, I must do something…say something.”

“What happened up north exactly?” asked Selene.

“Oh, it was terrible,” said Rosalie. “I was mortified. Ashamed. The trial was messy and public with the media waiting for lurid details. Of course, he was found guilty of sexual abuse,” said Rosalie, hiding her face with her hands. “The girls were frightened and scared because he was their priest so never said anything. But one of them finally spoke out. After that, many, many young women told stories of the same thing from him. Many had abortions. This abuse had been going on for years and years, back thirty years or more! He got away with it because he was a priest. I am disgusted. We are all disgusted. When he was found guilty, he was immediately deported. And now, here he is.”

During Rosalie’s rant against her uncle, Selene had been watching her. And Carlos. They both looked distraught. When the Mexican beauty finally paused, Selene asked, “does anyone here in Progreso know this? Aside from your family, I mean?”

Both Carlos and Rosalie shook their heads. “We hope not,” said Carlos quietly.

“How old is your uncle? Can he work at all? I mean, is he physically fit?”

“What would you say, Rosalie? He must be over 50 now. Grey hair. Soft body…by that I mean he has no muscles. Not used to hard labour at all.”

For one millisecond, Selene almost suggested in a sick way that he should take over the street clown act begun by Carlos. But she knew that was beyond cruel. And was immediately ashamed she even had that thought.

"I do not know the job situation here at all," said Selene.

"Believe me," replied Carlos. "It's bad. Unless you own your own business. And even that's iffy cuz you need investment money which no-one has. Fishing is the link for most people here. That's even a crazy thing to consider for him. He knows nothing about the sea. Or fishing. He joined the church when he was a teen -- my grandfather was so proud of him -- and he's done nothing but be a priest until now."

"What about you, Rosalie?" Selene turned to her. "Do you know anything about him that will help?"

"Nothing," said the beauty. "What's worse, I want to return to my job in Canada so I really don't want anything more to do with him. I just felt I should come back to help with some sort of adjustments."

While Rosalie was talking, a crazy idea popped into Selene's head. She couldn't shake it. After all, she hadn't even met this 'defrocked' priest!

"Carlos," she turned to face him, "I know this is going to sound nuts but what if I could find some menial tasks for him to do at the eco-resort?

We couldn't pay much if anything. Probably an honorarium. But maybe it would help restore some personal pride, keep him out of your mother's hair, maybe he'd find a skill he didn't know he had, maybe…maybe…." She paused.

Carlos's face was difficult to read. Then,

"You ARE crazy, Selene. Absolutely not. Can you imagine Mike's reaction? Besides, what can he do? He's so used to be catered to, he's useless. And I would personally feel so uncomfortable knowing he was there. In your space. No! This is a crazy idea, Selene. Absolutely."

Now it was Rosalie's turn.

"Wait a minute, Selene. I do not know your place at all but the fact you are willing to offer him something, anything, would be a tremendous boost to his morale. I bet he'd do anything for you. After all, Carlos," and she turned to her cousin, "we don't know what he can or can't do manually. We're assuming he's hopeless."

Then, before Carlos could utter a word, Selene said, "So, it's settled. I just need to talk with Mike first." She got up to go.

Carlos grabbed her, hard, on the arm. "I said, no," he repeated harshly. "And I meant it."

Selene looked at the welt beginning to swell on her upper arm with alarm. "Good grief, Carlos, what the hell you do that for?" Rosalie looked surprised. Agitated. And that's when the new plan suddenly came to Selene. She quickly sat down again, ignoring Carlos who was holding his head in his hands.

"Okay," she began. "Maybe I was too hasty but that's me. Here's another idea...." And she looked at Rosalie. Carlos had dropped his hands, ready to listen. They both turned to Selene.

"Rosalie, you are one beautiful young woman," Selene began. "In fact, until I found out you were Carlos's cousin, I was quite jealous watching you two together...." She paused.

"Mike loves beautiful women. And although Carlos thinks otherwise, Mike and I are NOT," she emphasized, "a couple. Yes, we live together. But we both know deep in our hearts that as a couple, we probably won't be one in the future." She watched each of her table companions, trying to see if they could understand where she was going with this....

"My idea now," she turned to Rosalie, "is quite simple. You come with your uncle to our Retreat under some pretense. I'll be sure not to be around. So, only Mike will be there. Your job, knowing how Mike enjoys attractive women -- and you've worked in Canada -- and you speak perfect English -- is somehow present your uncle to Mike as someone who needs a second chance in life. Mike likes to think he's a saviour of lost souls...like me, for instance. That you'll be happy to act as a go-between...that you heard this eco-retreat was starting up...."

"Wait a minute..." interrupted Rosalie.

"Play it by ear, Rosalie, play it by ear," grinned Selene, continuing. "I bet Mike offers a job to your uncle so long as somehow you're connected...."

And, thought Selene, I can stay connected to Carlos.

Chapter Nineteen

When Tommy finally opened his eyes, he was surprised and shocked to find he was lying in a hospital bed with fluids flowing through tubes hooked-up to a stand. His head ached. And he felt woozy. Like he had a hangover.

It took some time for his eyes to focus on the surroundings. Finally, he made out the outline of someone sitting beside his bed.

"You awake, Tommy?"

Copley's voice.

"What the hell am I doing here?" he snarled, dazed and doped.

"You tell me, cuz. One of the nurses here knew we were related and so called me after the paramedics brought you in."

Tommy lay silent.

"What happened, Tommy? You got an awful crack on the head. Nurses say you have a concussion."

Tommy's mind began to rewind. He frowned. "My head hurts."

"No kidding. But how'd this happen? Accident? Although the doc says looks as if you were attacked."

Tommy closed his eyes. He felt the bandages behind his left ear. And he hated to admit what he was about to say.

"MJ."

Copley's eyes popped wide open. Maybe he couldn't see them but Tommy knew that's exactly what Copley's blue eyes were doing. He sensed the shock on Copley's face.

"MJ?!"

"Look, don't wanna talk about it right now. Takes all my energy to say this much."

He closed his eyes. Could hear Copley's rapid breathing. It was bugging him.

"Oh, shut up, Cop!" Tommy spit out, his head splitting with pain.

"For Chrissake, Tommy! You gonna lay charges? You gonna....?"

"Shut up, Copley!"

Then in a more conciliatory tone: "Look, Cop. I'm feeling ragged. Do me a favour. Come back tomorrow if I'm still here. You and me's gonna make some plans."

"Sure, Tommy, sure." *Except*, thought Copley, *I've got a business to run. I have a partner who might not like Tommy's plans. And I sure as hell won't like whatever Tommy's got on his mind.* Still, he kept wondering, *what does all this have to do with MJ?*

He glanced again at his neck/head-bandaged
cousin. Tommy was out like a light. This time
Copley chose to leave the hospital room. He'd come
again tomorrow. The nurse told him that, depending
on how Tommy was then, a decision would be
made about his release. She also filled in some
blanks Copley had about Tommy's injury.

She explained a concussion was a temporary
injury to the brain caused by a sudden bump or
blow to the head. It usually lasts only a few days or
weeks. Sometimes a concussion needs emergency
treatment, like Tommy's, and some people can have
longer-lasting problems. Doctors wanted to keep an
eye on Tommy for awhile.

When Copley left the hospital, he was on
edge. Somehow, he knew he was being drawn into
something he did not want. And what the hell did
MJ have to do with any of this? Surely, she wasn't
the one who hit him! Was she?

Then his brain began to churn…

For sure, Copley definitely did not want to
get involved with Tommy and MJ's relationship. He
knew MJ was practically a prisoner and he knew it
was because of Tommy's insecurities. He also knew
MJ had changed significantly from the teen-aged
girl rescued from the streets years ago by Tommy,
to the young woman -- all this time later -- who had
obviously self-educated herself at the library and
developed into a strong-willed and – if he admitted
to his gay self – attractive woman. It was only a
matter of time, he reasoned, when MJ would make a
break for it. He was pretty sure she had suffered all

these years from the Stockholm Syndrome: he knew it happens to some abuse and hostage victims when they develop positive feelings towards their captor.

So did she? he wondered. Was she the one who cracked him over his head? And where the hell could she go? Tommy would follow her like a hound dog. He wouldn't rest until he got his hands on her again. And then God help her.

Copley shuddered.

Then there was this open-ended statement that Tommy had muttered before Copley left his cousin's hospital room: "You and me gonna make plans….." Copley was not a happy camper. What the hell did all this mean? He was not a fan of Tommy and could never be.

To be fair, he remembered when they were growing up…and this being a small town and all…how Copley was teased unmercifully because he was gay. He was always being accosted by bullies, hated to leave the house. Worse, he knew he was a disappointment to his super straight parents.

And who came to his rescue every time? Cousin Tommy! Big, bad, mean Tommy was always protecting him. Fending off the mean ones. Loved having an excuse for violence. Using his fists, he fought while Copley disappeared. *Run, Cop, run!* Tommy would yell as he began pummeling a tyrant. And Copley ran, terrified, to a safe place.

But that was then and this was now. Since those painful years, Copley had done his share of

114

living. He left Brighton after university to travel the world carrying a backpack and an open mind. Copley started in Europe (thank goodness for its well-developed train system), hit Thailand's island beaches, and then, met David, from Brighton in England ("what are the chances of us both coming from a Brighton on different continents?") in an airport on the way to Crete. David wanted to visit the caves of Zeus. He invited Copley to join him. Together the two visited the port of Chania where they stayed a few months learning to cook Greek food with a local chef and exploring the Greek ruins of Knossos. And the caves of Zeus.

By the time David suggested they 'hop' the Atlantic for Mexico and the Maya ruins – another ancient civilization – Copley sensed they would remain together as a couple. A sudden peace enveloped both of them. Admitted Copley to his partner, "I couldn't be happier."

When the couple hit the Yucatán Peninsula of Mexico, where the roots of the Maya civilization lay embedded in the ruins of Dzibilchaltun, Chichen Itza, Uxmal, Palenque, and other classical sites, they became fascinated with – and ardent students of -- Maya history. Both settled down in the seaside fishing town of Progreso on The Gulf of Mexico where they remained for four months, learning Spanish and appreciating the culture of the area.

And when it felt time to move on, Copley suggested to David that he come with him to Brighton, Ontario. They opened the perfect small business together and continued to travel. They chose to produce and perfect the best french fries in town in their mortgaged chip truck, the most popular snacking spot in Brighton's beachfront park at the edge of the river. A perfect combination for them: work hard during the summer, travel hard during the winter.

For once, Copley felt in charge of his life. He and David were an openly gay couple, seemingly accepted by a more mind-expanding community of the present day.

But there was a stickler, and Copley knew it:

Tommy.

Chapter Twenty

Paralyzed with fear, MJ remained uncannily silent as Alex steered his white Ford compact towards the Canadian/US border crossing from Fort Erie, Ontario, to Buffalo, New York.

She was terrified. She'd made her break -- and with her childhood sweetheart -- but had no idea what would happen next. She had no plan, no clothes, little idea where she was headed, and her anxiety level was at an all-time high. The only thing she did know was that the baby hole in her heart was thumping madly. For some irrational reason, she knew she was doing the right thing. And with the right person. But the fear of Tommy loomed so large in her mind, she thought she'd scream.

"Alex," she finally simpered, "I'm not sure I can do this. I feel terrible you've been forced into this escape," she floundered. "I don't know what I'm doing or why I'm doing it. No, wait," she admonished herself, "I do know. I'm just shocked at what I've done, that I've gotten you involved in something hideous, and that we're both in danger. I know Tommy. He won't stop until he kills us both."

Alex glanced over at her. "MJ," he said with determination, "We've gone over all this. You have not forced me into anything I didn't want to do."

Eyes focused on the QEW highway, he continued, "All these years you've put up with this monster because he's had you under his thumb. Your overriding prayer has been to find your daughter. You have reasonable proof she might be in the Yucatán in Mexico. You are going to try and find her. You needed someone to take you. That's me. The guy who hasn't stopped loving you since grade school." He looked over at her quickly with a warm smile, spreading his hand reassuringly over hers. "It's my decision to drive you."

"Yes, but we don't know what's happened to Tommy, do we?" she half-whispered. "What if I killed him? Then I'll be charged with murder…."

"Stop it, MJ," ordered Alex. "You were defending me. There isn't a victim of his in town who wouldn't testify about his brute force if it came to that. But it won't."

Then he added, "we'll stop in Cleveland. Do a bit of shopping for clothes and things. There's a Macy's there and lots of specialty shops. Let's just get across the border."

And then suddenly, the Peace Bridge connecting Fort Erie with Buffalo, NY, loomed large before them.

To MJ's surprise, there was no issue crossing the border into the U.S. Alex simply told the truth. They were driving through the U.S. and heading directly to Mexico. "Leaving anything in the U.S.?" the customs officer barked after checking their passports.

"No, sir," replied Alex.

After a cursory glance in the car, he waved them on. MJ released a long sigh, realizing only then how uptight she had been.

After overnighting in Cleveland, they stopped the next morning at Legacy Village where MJ purchased on credit some necessary clothing: underwear, nightwear, face creams, tee shirts, sandals and shorts.

As they headed out to continue their drive south, Alex turned to MJ: "I need to check in with Steve from the store. Maybe we'll hear what's happened to Tommy."

"Do you have to?" Her heart hammered at the mention of Tommy.

"It's okay, MJ. We need to find out and I need to keep Steve in the loop here. I can trust him. He's been with me for years."

Alex caught Steve at his home. His brief conversation was all business with a final question: "So what happened to that guy we called 911 for?"

Watching Alex's face, MJ could not guess.

"What happened?" she breathlessly asked after Alex cut the call.

Alex turned to her. "Well, he was picked up by ambulance and taken to the hospital…."

"And…?"

"He's in hospital now with a mild concussion. Steve says when some people in town found out about it, the general consensus was almost one of admiration, *'how did anyone ever get the chance to attack Tommy?'*

MJ winced. Alex threw his arms around her shoulder and squeezed her close.

"Let's get moving, kiddo," he said as they reached the car in the shopping centre parking lot.

****

Alex showed MJ his planned routing since he needed her help navigating the most direct drive to the Mexican border. He had already pinpointed the crossing they would take at Brownsville in Texas to Matamoros, Tamaulipas, in Mexico.

He pulled into a motel along Interstate 90 on their way to Cleveland, Ohio, for the night. MJ was uncharacteristically quiet during the drive. That's because her brain and heart were not in sync. She sighed openly, wept sometimes, squirmed in her seat, shoved her hands over her face.

"Relaxed, are you?" he half-joked as they pulled into the motel.

MJ turned to Alex. "I'm an internal mess! Keep asking myself what am I doing here? Why do I think any daughter I had over twenty years ago would want her real mother to suddenly show up? What if this girl is not my Maya? Or in Mexico? Chances are she's not. What the hell am I doing dragging you into it? And now I'm terrified Tommy will somehow find us…" she glanced sidelong at Alex. "No, I'm not relaxed."

120

"Hey, MJ," soothed Alex. "Easy for me to say not to worry. But what if you didn't take this chance? What if you stayed in Brighton the rest of your life? What if...."

"Enough!" and MJ put up her hand to stop him. "Let's just both agree I'm a mess. No more what if's...."

Thankfully, thought MJ as Alex unlocked the door to their room, there were twin beds. She had no desire for desire. And to Alex's credit, he must have assumed as much.

That night as she looked into the motel bathroom mirror, she had a conversation with herself. Decided she was going to make a go of it and thank God Alex was making no demands. In fact, he was perfect, letting her stew alone in her own mental anguish.

"Let's go, then," said MJ in the morning after a sleepless night. All she had heard from Alex during the night was his long, slow breathing rhythm -- like an innocent babe -- while MJ lay wide awake shattered in pieces.

As the miles lengthened between Brighton and her current destinations, MJ began to look ahead. Not behind.

So, it was on to southern Ohio. Then Kentucky where they ran into dense fog in the early morning hours on their way south to Louisville. In Tennessee, they stopped to eat at Loretta Lynn's kitchen/dude ranch along the Music Highway. Once they arrived in Memphis, both devoured pulled pork at B.B. King's on famous Beale Street. Alex ordered bourbon on the rocks because it seemed appropriate to drink bourbon in a blues bar on Beale. MJ began to relax a little.

They crossed the Mississippi into Arkansas, home to former U.S. President Bill Clinton.

Gradually she began to breathe normally. That baby hole in her heart had stopped burning. And MJ felt that somewhere along this trip with Alex, she needed to tell him the truth about Maya, how she had gotten pregnant, and her subsequent bad life choices.

She glanced at him as he sang along with an Eagles' tune on Sirius and realized he really must love her. Or at least deeply care for her. He seemed to be happy just to be in her company. Despite all the complications. He called his manager, Steve, daily: to get news about the business but also about Tommy. By now Alex had clued Steve into Tommy's attack on him and MJ's attack on Tommy. As far as Steve knew, Tommy was still in hospital. But he suspected he would be released soon.

As for MJ, she allowed herself to think about living again. She began to think this Maya project at the LES in Mérida might be just the thing to keep her mind intellectually honed. She was looking forward to it and to meeting the young woman with whom she would be working. The greater the distance from Canada, the more relaxed she felt. Who knows what adventures awaited? And her daughter....? MJ took a deep breath.

They had been on the road for 3 days now.

Turning to Alex, she began to share her thoughts with him. She couldn't help notice he'd been uncharacteristically quiet for the past day or so.

"Whatcha thinkin' Alex?" she asked.

"'Bout Steve."

"Steve? Why? What's the matter with Steve?"

"That's just it, MJ. I haven't heard from him. He's usually pretty punctual with a call once a day. It's been almost two days now."

"Really? Gosh, I guess I hadn't noticed."

"I have."

Silence.

"Why do you suppose that is?"

"Not sure, MJ. But I'm feeling uncomfortable about it."

"Well, why not call him?"

"The agreement was he'd call me every day or else let me know why."

MJ began to fidget. Alex was sounding worried. That wasn't Alex unless he felt something was wrong.

"Why don't you call him?" she suggested.

"As soon as we cross into Texas that's exactly what I'm going to do." He turned and smiled.

They crossed into Texas at Texarkana; the Mexican border loomed closer. But Texas is a large state and it would take forever to cover it. Alex drily commented, "you know…I'm more concerned about guns in Texas than I will be in Mexico…"

He stopped at a gas bar, filled up, then drove over to the side of the business to park. "Think I'll give Steve a shout."

For some reason MJ felt her heart beat faster. Maybe it was Alex's serious attitude. Maybe it was fear of hearing what Steve might say…

"Funny. No answer," said Alex, frowning. "This would be a slow time at the store…"

Suddenly, he waved off MJ's distracting questions. His call had been answered. "shhh" he motioned to her. "…Steve…?" MJ could hear a male voice.

Then a maniacal laugh.

Then a disconnect.

Chapter Twenty-One

Mike had just returned to the eco retreat from his beach run, showered, hastily brewed a coffee, and was just sitting down with it in his hands at the front desk, when he heard the knock.

"Come in," he answered.

He did not expect to see this beautiful young woman – obviously Mexican with her long jet-black hair tied back into a loose ponytail – who cautiously opened the door.

He smiled warmly. "What can I do for you?"

"Oh, excuse me," she replied in her lilting English/Spanish accent, "I was looking for the owner of theese place."

"You got him. My name's Mike." He held out his hand to shake her delicate one while holding her dark eyes with his hazel ones. "And yours…."

"Oh, how I hope you can help me…..my name ees Rosalie."

And she launched into her tale of woe. "I hope you do not think me too forward to come here. I have read about this new place in the *Diario*." She paused.

Intrigued, Mike nodded for her to continue. "You speak English very well…are you from around here?"

Rosalie sighed deeply. "I live in Canada actually." She noticed his eyes widening with interest. And then she launched into her well-rehearsed spiel before he could ask any more questions.

"I feel so embarrassed barging in like this...but I have an uncle, living here now, who used to live in Canada, and now he needs help."

Mike sat up straighter, his mind churning, suspicious. Was he being taken for a scam here? What was this stunning-looking young woman suddenly in his office with some sob story about her uncle? He was not into charity cases.

"Please hear me out," she begged as her beautiful dark eyes, outlined with beautifully long black eyelashes, studied the skeptical expression on his face. His warm smile had morphed into a frown.

He knew he couldn't refuse to listen. He also knew how susceptible he was to the charms of attractive young women. And this one was a looker with a most attractive Spanish accent.

So, he listened. With reservations.

When she finished, out of breath, he stood up. Walked to the coffee machine. Turned to her sitting earnestly in front of his desk and offered: "coffee?"

She shook her head. He could tell she was all business and this was important business for her.

"First, Rosalie, you should understand we haven't even thought of hiring help. Second, we aren't open right now. And most important, I wouldn't have the faintest idea of what to do with a defrocked priest even if we needed helpers here."

He watched as she bit her luscious lower lip. Damn, he thought, she invokes his carnal sensibilities!

"Perhaps I am too hasty. I just thought I would be first to approach you for hiring help because I must return to my job in Canada and I wanted so much to have my uncle looked after."

"But why me? More important…you tell me he was found guilty of sexually abusing girls? What makes you think I would even consider a criminal?"

"Yes," she bit that lower lip again, "I am so ashamed to speak about him like this to you, a stranger, but I am desperate. I cannot speak to people in town. They would scorn him. Not help him. And right now, he needs help."

"If I may say so, Rosalie," and here Mike approached her, fixing his eyes on hers, "I find it extraordinary you think I would even consider taking him on. And to do what?"

Her hands were twisting in her lap. "A hands-on worker? Or, a professional counsellor on staff for guests who might like to talk about their problems? Everyone has problems! Or, he could teach Spanish? I had the idea that offering Spanish lessons at your retreat might entice a higher paying guest…." She stopped, breathing hard.

Mike looked at – no -- stared at her. She was visibly upset, almost crying. Oh gawd, he thought, why the hell did I invite her in?!

"Does he have any qualifications other than raping little girls?" he quietly demanded.

She flashed her dark eyes at him.

"And why would I even consider a defrocked priest in my place? Do I look like an idiot? I'm trying to start up a first-class tourist business in this God-forsaken fishing village and you suggest I hire your disgraced uncle? Like, I just don't get it!"

Suddenly, she blurted out: "I met your partner."

Mike's face turned to stone.

"And she gave me hope that you might consider giving him a chance…" Rosalie didn't get very far when Mike interrupted.

"You met Selene? Where? When? How?" His churning thoughts came quickly. Suddenly his demeanour changed from ingratiating warmth to hanging icicles. He tried to hide the shift.

"Oh, I met her with Carlos in *Amigos*…."

It was all Mike could do to maintain an even tone. Even though Rosalie was attractive, the thought of Selene meeting with Carlos in the expat bar was enough to raise his blood pressure to a dangerous level. He knew, though, he had to remain calm. To get more information. To figure out how and why Selene was with Carlos at all!

"So what did Selene suggest that brings you here? I haven't seen my partner lately so I'm not sure what she was thinking…"

Encouraged by his supposed interest, Rosalie blathered on…

"We were discussing my uncle and his situation and she merely mentioned there might be an opportunity for him to work here since you guys are just starting up…And I need to get back to my job in Ottawa…."

"Ottawa?"

"Yes. You know….Canada's capital."

"That's where Selene and I met. Is your defrocked uncle from Ottawa too?"

"Uh, no," she replied with soft brown eyes. "He was a priest in Brighton, not far from…"

"Brighton, Ontario? About an hour from Ottawa?" pressed Mike.

"Yes." Rosalie stopped talking. She was running on empty and didn't know what to say next.

While Mike slowly studied her with eyes wide open now, he was thinking. About Brighton. About the fact he had distant disdained family in that small town. In fact, if he stretched his mind a bit, he had older cousins there that he knew about but had never met. And didn't want to meet. Some gay clown who ran a chip wagon and a town bully who ran a carpenter shop. And a family rumour that the bully, name of Tommy, was guilty of keeping a woman against her will. Coincidentally, this defrocked priest from Brighton, Ontario, related to this beautiful babe in front of him, needs a job. Even more coincidental, Mike knew his mom had been cheated out of family money by this Tommy guy. Small world, thought Mike wryly, as his mind raced with ideas. What if he did hire this defrocked priest and pried some Brighton information out of him? It's possible, he thought. It's possible. Family money, he surmised, might be forthcoming after all. And priests know everything about their flock. Especially one found guilty of sexually abusing little girls.

Rosalie was sitting, sweating, in front of him. She studied him in his silence. He was virile, attractive, obviously clever, and a risk taker. She understood Selene's attraction to him. She felt the same way.

Suddenly Mike stirred. He ran his fingers around his face, thinking. Turned to look at her beautiful beseeching face.

"Maybe, Rosalie," he finally said, "we can work something out."

Chapter Twenty-Two

It didn't take Tommy long to recover. With proper medical care and a desire to get back to normal, he decided his first task was to find MJ and drag her home. Or kill her. Right now, he didn't care about anything else. His was a twisted diabolical mind; he reasoned that since MJ had tried to kill him with that poker, he was merely paying her back. Only he would succeed. His lips curled up at the corners into an evil grin. Maybe this would be even more fun than trying to keep her locked up.

"You've taken on the wrong guy, MJ," he snarled to himself. "Now, to find out where you've gone with that wimpy creep and how to get you." He delighted in imagining the horror on her face when he finally found her.

First, however, he needed to find out where she went. *Easy enough*, he thought. *I'll just mosey on over to that men's store where MJ almost killed me. Bet someone there knows.*

And that's where he found Steve, legs up on his desk, reading a newspaper. No-one else around.

"Hi there," greeted the salesman, Steve, folding his newspaper and standing up to greet this muscle-bound man with a well-bandaged ear standing too near him. He offered his hand. "Steve's the name. How can I help you?"

"Looking for the owner," Tommy snorted.

"Why, I'm sorry, Mr… what did you say your name was…? The owner's away on business right now. Can I help you?"

"I need to speak to the owner. Now."

"Well, gee, I'm sorry, sir. He's away on business."

"Where?"

"Not sure, sir. He just asked me to fill in here for him for a few days."

Tommy grabbed Steve's collar. "Well, *Steve-baby*, I need to talk with your boss now!"

Steve tried to pull away. "I'm not sure how to reach him, I'm sorry."

"You'll be a lot sorrier if I don't get to speak with him NOW," threatened Tommy. "Let's make this real easy. Surely you keep connected by cell…"

Steve's fear gave way to action. He pulled out his cell and auto-dialled Alex's private number. He watched Tommy's face as both men heard Alex saying "hello…hello…Steve…?"

Tommy let out a maniacal laugh. Then he disconnected the call.

Steve stared into this madman's cold eyes. He was in no mood to be a hero.

"He's on his way to Mexico," he said. "Now please leave. I have other customers waiting."

****

The next stop Tommy made was at the library. He walked straight over to Glenda, that pretty little lady whose face he would smash if she didn't give him the information he wanted.

"MJ's gone," he hissed into her frightened face when he caught up with her between shelves.

"Well, I wondered what happened, Tommy," she answered smoothly. "She hasn't turned up for a few days - I was about to call you."

"Like hell. You damn well know where she is, or is going, and if you don't tell me right now, I'll destroy your pretty little face. Here and now."

Tommy saw her eyes flicker with fear. "And don't tell me she's on her way to Mexico. I know that already. I want to know exactly *where* in that god-forsaken country."

Glenda bit her lip. Cast her eyes down.

"She's going to a city in the Yucatán," she said curtly and turned her back on him to rearrange some shelving.

Tommy had only one more piece of business to tend to. He went to the chip truck to find Copley.

"Cop," he demanded, "where'd you say you spent some time in Mexico with your gay buddy?"

Copley glanced fearfully at his partner. "Yucatán Peninsula. Why?"

"You and me's gonna take a little trip, cuz. As soon as we can."

****

It didn't take long before Tommy convinced Copley to leave his chip wagon in the care of his partner. Copley never stood a chance. Still, he tried.

"What makes you think Mary Jane is in Mexico and why would I go with you?"

Tommy ignored the first part of the question. Instead he said quietly with conviction: "Cuz you owe me money for that chip truck and cuz you and me always did things together. Since kids."

Copley thought of his personal life and his partner, Dave, and how he and Dave had started to feel comfortable together as a couple lately in this small town where everyone knows everyone and being gay isn't easy.

"And if I don't want to do this?" asked Copley.

Despite holding a psychology degree, Tommy still believed the best method of persuasion was brute force. Probably why he never made use of his degree and instead opened a carpenter shop in Brighton. He was talented with his hands when he used them constructively rather than threatening Mary Jane or someone else.

"I need you with me, Cop. You speak Spanish and I don't. And I trust few people but I do trust you."

So Copley, against his will but powerless to refuse his crazed cousin, flew with Tommy to Mérida, capital city of the Yucatán, on a mission of revenge.

Chapter Twenty-Three

In absolute mental agony, MJ sat forlornly beside Alex while they argued about when to try and reach Steve again. Both knew the crazy laugh belonged to Tommy. MJ froze at the sound; Alex was angry. Their constant see-saw discussion meant the long drive through Texas passed quickly. Crazy scenarios took over their bored minds.

Finally, having covered 1,864 miles (3000 km) from the Canadian/US border to Brownsville, TX, across from Matamoros, Mexico, they reached the Mexican border. Before Alex had a chance to stop and text him, Steve called from Brighton.

"The evil man was here yesterday," reported his manager. "I didn't dare call you until at least today. He's looking for the girl. And frankly, Alex, it's a good thing you're out of the country. He'd kill as soon as talk with you. I was, quite frankly, terrified. And he knows you're going to Mexico. My mistake there. But I didn't want him to take out one of my eyes."

"He ask anything else?"

"No. He seemed to think that was all the info he needed. Look, be careful, Alex. I know you're far away but this guy is poison."

"Thanks, buddy. I know what you're saying. Just keep in touch when you can, please. I think he won't bother you anymore if he got the info he wanted." Call ended.

MJ looked straight ahead. "We're screwed now, Alex. He's going to come after us," she declared matter-of-factly. "I know his diabolical mind. He's not going to stop until he kills me. Kills us both."

"Look, MJ," said Alex. "Let's not get ahead of ourselves. Mexico is a big country. He won't know where you are…"

"Why don't I believe that…?"

"Anyway, let's cross the border, get going. We've got to believe everything will be OK."

****

Since their processing took only about 20 minutes, Alex and MJ considered themselves lucky. Mind you, the female officer was no help. Her name tag said Sandra, and MJ referred to her as 'Sullen Sandra'. She pouted as she went about her work, frowning at Alex's credit card, speaking only Spanish when both Alex and MJ knew she was bilingual. They decided Sandra was the perfect border bureaucrat.

They had to make copies of all their documents: passports, car ownership, credit cards, driver's license, visa and so on. Sullen Sandra ceremoniously directed them to two guys at the *copias* desk who dutifully made the copies and then slyly asked: 'you can make a donation to help pay for the copies if you want'. Alex parted with two American dollars. The clerks looked at the donation and grunted.

So now, thought MJ in amazement and uncertainty, she was actually in Mexico. Matamoros, Mexico to be exact, directly across the narrow, dirty Rio Grande from Brownsville, Texas. Right away she noticed the difference. The Mexican town was dirty, dusty, crowded, with *mucho Carta Blanca* beer signs.

Now they were driving in the open countryside. The landscape was surprisingly cultivated, unlike its counterpart in Texas. Little *casas* were painted in pastel shades of lime green, turquoise, bright blue, and a Dandelion gold. Chickens scurried about the dirt; burros and donkeys were tethered close to the road where they cropped the grass. Herds of cattle, goats and sheep roamed the fields near the *autopista*.

Driving deeper and deeper into this strange new land of tamales, being conscious of suspect vehicles, they were also aware of drug cartel gangs…although they had been assured at the border that this part of Mexico did not suffer from cartel attacks.

"Although that's not what our government believes," muttered Alex. "We better keep our eyes open and our hands on the wheel" ready to outmanoeuvre any weird attempts by strangers.

As the days wore on, the weather changed dramatically. Expecting nothing but hot, sunny days, they were dismayed when rain began to plague their trip.

"Think we better stop at a motel and stay a few days," suggested Alex. "Looks like some flooding in the fields around here and I'm not prepared for any emergencies."

Both spied the Best Western Brisa, a popular chain on the gulf side of Mexico, as they turned off the highway into Coatzacoalcos, a small city bordering the sea. Alex waited for the rain to ease before entering the office. Fierce winds drove torrential rains like sheets of water. Palm tree fronds swung in wild abandon, their tree trunks wrapped in protective layers of burlap.

Because stranded travellers filled the hotel, they were lucky to find one available room. Another phenomenon, however, jolted their sensibilities even more when they drove into the courtyard. Everywhere they looked they saw *federales*: police from the Mexican Government's special force units. Dressed in black attack regalia, wearing flak jackets, gloves, dark sun shades despite the rain, and holding uzis, they looked fearsome and for MJ, a shudder of alarm ran up and down her back. They counted 11 of them in sight. One of them, perched at the door of the hotel, looked her over in too much detail.

Settling into their dim little room, Alex decided to nap after the rigorous drive along the highway. MJ was too agitated to sit for long. "I'll be outside," she murmured to Alex. "I think the rain is letting up."

As she closed the door to their room, she spotted one of the *federales* at the poolside table under the *palapa,* a thatched roof made of dried palm leaves. He was in full uniform with his uzi slung comfortably across his knee. Because of their presence, she was beginning to feel the hotel guests were in some kind of a witness protection program. As she passed, the *federale* nodded, said "good afternoon". MJ looked back at him. "Good afternoon. You speak English?"

"Yes," he said. "You are from Canada? I see the Ontario licence." His fixed look met hers and something inside MJ clicked as their eyes momentarily locked together. Embarrassed, she quickly averted her eyes.

"If there is anything you'd like to know, señora, just ask me. I am at your service." She thanked him, about to walk on and then suddenly turned back.

"The *autopista* to Mérida. Is it open yet?"

"No," he replied emphatically. "It is not. You are safer here."

MJ found herself drawn to him. She held out her hand. "My name is Mary Jane but everyone calls me MJ. Your name is.....?"

He carefully placed the uzi beside him on the poolside table as he held out his hand to shake and said, "Roberto. My name is Roberto and I can't believe you have driven all the way from Ontario to this place." He smiled warmly.

"You know where Ontario is?" she asked.

"I lived for 20 years in New York City."

"Ah, that explains your excellent English, Roberto."

He smiled, an open, honest smile, and she completely forgot he was clothed in attack gear or that an uzi lay ominously beside him.

"Please," he said. "Feel free to sit down. It's dry under the umbrella. It is not often I have a chance to speak English and with such a pretty lady." When he spoke, his words and tone were genuine and MJ felt an instant attraction.

"What are you doing here? You and all your, uh, well-equipped friends?" She laughed at her unintended pun that passed over Roberto's head.

"We're actually on a break. An R&R break," he said. "But even on a break we must constantly be on guard against drug gangs," he explained. "We've been up in the hills for a time and now with so many of us in one place, we are vulnerable. One of our men in another unit was shot and killed not many days ago. These drug guys are ruthless and will not hesitate to attack wherever we are."

"That's awful," she said. "If, by horrible chance, the drug lords come gunning for you in this hotel, would the guests also be in danger?"

"I cannot say for sure, but, probably, yes."

MJ thought about that. She watched some of the off duty *federales* laugh and shout in the pool as they horsed around in the light drizzle. Roberto followed her gaze.

"At the end of our shifts, we jump into the pool and play like children," he said. "We don't mind the rain."

MJ looked at him. "You are very brave." She didn't mean for swimming in the rain. He understood her comment.

"No," he said. "You and your man are very brave to drive through Mexico like you are."

"He's not my man," said MJ seriously. "But he is a close friend. What do you mean we are brave to drive through Mexico? Do we have anything to fear?"

"Probably not. Only if you are in the wrong place at the wrong time. You do not want to do anything foolish."

"Like......?" MJ's eyebrows shot up.

Roberto shrugged.

They sat in comfortable silence, Roberto's hand back on his uzi and his eyes on the courtyard door. "Why did you leave New York?" she asked, remembering her own border crossing with Alex only a few days ago. *Did we really cross only a few days ago?* she thought.

Time passed as MJ heard Roberto's story and she, surprisingly, shared her real story with him. *Isn't that what they say*, she mused silently. *You tend to share your life story with strangers because they are non-judgmental. And you'll never see them again.*

She thought Roberto's story very tragic. He returned to Mexico because his father, an innocent bystander, was killed in a shoot-out between rival drug gangs. That's what he meant, he explained, when he said being in the wrong place at the wrong time. He came to help his distraught mother, then fell in love and married Christina, an intelligent investigative journalist. She, too, was shot by members of a drug gang, only this time Roberto was sure she was targeted because of her in-depth articles on the drug war. He felt the only option open to him was to join the *federales* and fight those responsible for the deaths of his father and wife.

For some reason, MJ opened up her heart to this stranger. When she finished her story: raped by a priest, forced to give up her daughter for adoption, falling into a destructive and controlling relationship for so many years, and now running away to search for her daughter with the help of good-hearted Alex, Roberto stopped her just as she became emotional.

He put aside his uzi for a moment and took her hand gently. "You are very brave, Señora MJ," he said with utmost tenderness. "You and I have lost our innocence and how we handle the rest of our lives will determine what kind of people we really are."

MJ accepted his hand into hers, looked into his dark passionate eyes, and said, "I can't believe I've told you all this. There has to be a reason we've met."

Chapter Twenty-Four

Mike took almost a sadistic pleasure in needling Selene about her part introducing ex-Father Martin Garcia into their lives.

"Let's get this straight," he mocked. "You, a heavy drinker…former one I mean…" as she glared at him, "meet Carlos the Clown in *Amigos,* where he and his stunning cousin are wondering what to do with their sexual predator former priest uncle. And you, under the guise of being helpful, suggest sending sexy Rosalie to me and plead the case for hiring the pedophilia priest. And to think I almost fell for it!" Mike is standing, shaking his head, looking at his feet.

"You know, Selene, if you had straight come out and asked me, we could have had a reasonable discussion. As it is, I think you were trying to defraud me. Deceive me. Hardly the foundation of a healthy partnership. You must have been drinking! Right?" When Mike wanted to, he could be a real asshole, someone who would stick-it-to-you because he enjoyed belittling people. Like he had belittled Selene when she was in her most confused (and vulnerable) state of recovery.

She decided she didn't want to play his game anymore. "Forget it, Mike. I made a bad decision. You can be sure it won't happen again." And she opened the door to the inner retreat heading to her room.

"Wait a minute, sweetheart," he mocked. "You haven't heard the ending. Ex-Father Martin Garcia is coming by later this afternoon for a chat on what we want him to do. So, partner, I need you here with me."

He could sense, maybe not see, her astonished reaction. She wheeled around.

"What? You just finished admonishing me for my stupidity and now you're telling me you're going to have him here? Doing what? Bless your bad behaviour?"

Just before she thrashed through the door, Mike said in a low voice. "It might work out for both of us, M."

She stopped in her tracks. "How so, big boy?"

Mike threw up his hands. "Okay. Okay. I've deserved this cold reaction from you. But I just couldn't let you think you got away with your blatant plan of helping out Carlos the Clown."

He knew he hit a nerve.

"Let's forget my bad manners, S. And I'll explain what I have in mind AFTER I got over the shock of you setting me up like that. However," he continued as she eyed him, "Rosalie is a beauty. I could go for her. For sure."

And so, Mike shared his plan. He discovered, he said, that the bad priest had looked after his flock ('maybe looked after is too weak a word for him, maybe fucked his flock is better' he

144

snorted) for many, many years in Brighton, his old
hometown. Selene eyed him curiously. She knew
about this town from his past and that Mike came
from there but there had never been any other
meaningful discussion.

"There's a little matter about a family
inheritance that I am entitled to but never received. I
have a bully cousin called Tommy living there who
terrified everyone challenging him in those days
when I grew up there. He even bullied my poor
mother who was afraid of her own shadow,
especially after dad died. She and her sister, who
actually threw her own daughter out of the house,
tried to take Tommy to court. But the judge was
found beaten to death. And suddenly, my mother
and aunt's lawyer dropped the case. This happened
years ago, I was just a kid, but I'm betting the bad
Father might have been privy to some personal and
private knowledge in the rotten neighbourhoods of
Brighton. Small pious town, you know. Confession
booths and all that."

Selene stared at Mike.

"I want to find out what the bad Father
knows. I'm willing to string him along, use his
priestly talents, and see what I can uncover." He
stopped. "So, Selene, you may have been trying to
help Carlos the Clown but you have also
inadvertently helped me. Thanks for having my
interests at heart."

Mike stopped. Strode over to where Selene
was standing. Grabbed her by her long, mahogany-
coloured hair, pulled it back, kissed her hard on the

mouth while holding down her arms, pressed his hard cock against her soft body, and whispered, "what Mikey wants, Mikey gets. And right now, Selene baby, Mikey wants you."

****

The fuck left Selene breathless. She didn't want to let Mike know that she had come, more than once, and with passion. She couldn't calm down. Couldn't stop her ecstasy.

"You came more than once, baby, didn't you?" he smiled. "You know we love each other, Selene, but we get more aroused after an argument. Love it…" and his voice trailed off.

Desperately wanting to rid herself of his blatant masculinity, brute strength and know-it-all attitude, she changed the subject quickly. "What is your plan for our defrocked Father?" she asked between pulling on her underwear over her sperm-soaked vagina, and finger-combing her long hair.

"Let's advertise him as our on-site professional counsellor. We can make up some impressive credentials…I'm sure he can help us with that. That we offer not only a back-to-the-earth experience but a real remedy for suffering souls. Something like that. Lots of moneyed people are looking for that kind of therapy stuff. I've invited Rosalie to bring him this afternoon. So we can meet with him together."

He saw her look of consternation. "And don't worry. I'm not going to fuck her." He smiled. "Yet."

Chapter Twenty-Five

So this was Mérida, thought Tommy. Capital city of the state of Yucatán that bordered the Gulf of Mexico. A large, crowded, hot, stuffy place that left him longing for a cold shower.

In a rental car from the airport, leaving the driving to Cuzin Copley, Tommy sat back and surveyed this traffic-crazy city of Mexicans and thought: *now that I'm here, how do I find my runaway woman?*

"Where we goin', Cop?"

"We're booked into *Casa del Balam,* House of the Jaguar, to you. It's central."

"Good thing you've been here before with your lover buddy," snorted Tommy.

Once at the hotel -- to Copley's surprise -- Tommy took instant control. At the check-in desk, he asked the clerk, "You speak English?"

"Si Meester Tommy."

"Good. We've just arrived. Obviously." He grinned. "Where do we meet other tourists? Know any places foreigners hang out?" Tommy slipped a few unnecessary pesos into the surprised clerk's palm.

"There is an English Library in *centro* a few blocks from here," said the clerk. "A lot of expats hang out in that area. And…." he continued. "a restaurant, *La Casa de Frida,* within walking distance, is a favourite among our guests."

Tommy turned to his cousin. "Guess where we're going for lunch," he said. "I'm hungry."

The *Frida* Restaurant, with its bright pink sign, was easy to find. Once inside, the décor hit the two men as shockingly different and feminine. They almost left. Until they spied a few busy tables plus one with a lone female gringo sitting by the window. She turned to look at them out of curiosity. Nodded in their direction.

"Hello," she smiled. "You guys look lost. Are you?"

"Hi," said Tommy. "Kind of nice to hear English spoken. Like back home."

"Where's home?" she asked.

"Canada," answered Tommy. "…Ontario."

"No kidding," said the woman. "We're practically neighbours. I'm originally from Ontario, too."

"Well, well, well," smiled a charming Tommy. "This calls for a minor celebration don't ya think? What about sharing a welcome drink with us?" And he moved an empty chair to her table. Copley did the same.

"Sorry, but I don't drink while on the job," she smiled. "But I'd be happy to share any local information with you both. What are you looking for?"

"We're not quite sure," said Tommy. "Allow me to introduce myself. The name's Tommy. And beside me here is my cousin Copley who has visited this area before. And yes, we are strangers to these here parts."

"Pleasure to meet you both. The name's Bonnie and I'm on my lunch break."

"You work here? A gringo works in this Mexican city?" asked a curious Copley remembering how difficult it had been for David and him to find anything to top up their finances years ago while here. "What do you do?"

"Actually," said Bonnie, "I'm lucky. I head the LES here…oh, that means the Library for English Speakers…we are almost **the** melting pot for English speakers in this area."

Suddenly, the words *English Library* hit Tommy like a rock. His interest in this Bonnie woman intensified. Looking her over for fucking material, he decided she wasn't bad-looking in an average sort of way. A little overweight. Wore a sleeveless low-cut white blouse tucked into a long, flowing skirt of printed tropical flowers, and flat sandals. Not his type, though, he said to himself.

While he studied her, his brain shifted to MJ and that high-and-mighty slut librarian, Glenda, at the Brighton library. The name *Library for English Speakers* resonated with him. Why? A tiny seed in the back of his brain began to grow. He remembers….ah, yes…MJ. He knew about this place because she had been so excited she even shared it with him. MJ had been thrilled when Bonnie, Head Librarian at LES, had tapped into her Maya history interest through the Glenda slut. Stretching his mind back even more, Tommy remembered something else. A 'Bonnie' had invited MJ to assist in developing a special Maya section in the LES! At that time, though, Tommy had no idea the LES was here. In Mérida. In the Yucatán.

Twitching in his chair, he gave Copley a swift kick under the table. That meant Copley was to shut up. Meanwhile, Tommy feigned interest in Bonnie and the LES to glean some important information. This chance meeting was a gift from heaven, he decided. Obviously, the gods were on his side.

"So, tell us about the LES…" he began, feigning great interest. "Do you have special exhibits? How many members do you have? Would we be welcome?" and on and on.

Flattered, Bonnie explained the format, the membership, (Tommy nodded and nodded, impatiently waiting for the info he wanted) and finally, special exhibits.

"Ah," said Tommy, "special exhibits…on what?"

"Well, I'm really excited about this one," she fluttered. "It's on the history of the Maya in this area, but more importantly, our aim is to establish a permanent exhibit in English, become *the* centre for Maya history in this state, introduce Maya principles, study their astronomy methods, health practices like their sweat houses (*temazcals),* medicinal herbs, everything....!" Bonnie was beyond excited.

Tommy cringed. He still wasn't getting the information he wanted!

"Sounds as if this will cost a lot of money. And manpower. Any outside help?" There. He finally got it out, hopefully without raising suspicions or alarm.

"Oh," Bonnie bubbled on..."I've got some state seed money and a couple of helpers..."

"Helpers?" He wanted to hone in.

"Yes, a young girl, educated in Canada and living here, and an older woman, arriving any day now, also from Canada. Both are set to start soon."

Tommy was beside himself with anxiety and suspense.

"Wouldn't it be funny, maybe strange, if we knew either of these women...? Sort of like our chance meeting today..."

Bonnie laughed. "Well, I know it's a small world but it can't be that small!"

"Try us," Tommy was getting impatient. Tired of this cat and mouse game. His mind was whirling...*just give me the goddamn names, woman, and then shut your mouth!*

Bonnie picked up his negative vibe immediately. Saw cold eyes that seemed to be warmer just a moment ago. Suddenly she didn't want to discuss her exciting venture anymore with this stranger who was almost demanding and very commanding.

"Uh, don't want to bore you both with all this stuff," she smiled sweetly. "How rude of me!"

Tommy was itching to scratch out her eyes. Instead, he ignored her comment, smiled as genuinely as he could and said "You were saying about your helpers…."

Bonnie knew now that she wanted to be rid of this macho man and his weaker skinny cousin. If, indeed, he was his cousin. Why would they possibly care about her affairs?

"Uh, one of them lives in Progreso and the other is arriving soon from Canada," she managed to say quickly. Then she smiled sweetly, "Don't want to give out any more information because things are still not settled. But you are welcome to come to the exhibit when it finally opens. Of course," she added with a fake smile, "I'm not sure how long you two gentlemen will be here. And," she glanced at her watch, "I've overstayed my lunch hour… So great meeting you both. Now I must go."

Chapter Twenty-Six

From the window of their motel room, Alex had watched, but not heard, the verbal exchange between MJ and this *federale* guy. However, he could read both of their body gestures, understood their language as if he was beside them, noticed MJ move closer to the guy, saw his protective arm hover over her shoulders and draw her near.

An uneasy feeling swept over him. How could this be possible? Was his mind assuming a connection that really wasn't there? Was he catastrophizing? Surely in the time MJ and this guy had met and chatted, there couldn't be more that that. Just a chat. And yet, why was he conjuring up these disturbing thoughts?

Continuing on this thread of thinking, Alex methodically ticked off why MJ's chance meeting with the *federale* was bothering him. *Number 1*, he told himself, *we are not married or connected legally in any way. Number 2, MJ has never said she loved me; Number 3, I offered to drive her to Mexico although that's what she wanted…but was it what I wanted? Yes, he answered himself, I was, still am, excited. This is an adventure for me. So, am I just assuming she loves me?*

He paused. He *was* assuming she loved him. But she never said that, though their lovemaking had been mutually salacious. Just then he saw MJ leave the *federale,* who brushed his mouth against her face, as she headed to the motel room. Moving to the desk where he had set up his computer, he sat down, just as she opened the door.

"Alex," she said. "Guess what? Roberto, the guy I was just talking to, says the road will reopen by tomorrow....and," she paused, "he and his unit will leave, too. While they were here, they were instructed to keep watch over everyone from this motel heading for Mérida. Just in case there is any cartel action. Which he doesn't expect. But isn't it great to know we have some protection?!"

MJ was excited, breathless.

"Ever occur to you their very presence might bring unwanted attention on us innocent travellers?" replied Alex. After his stinging reply, Alex turned back quickly to his computer.

"Like, what's the matter with you, Alex? Here we have bona fide protection from Mexican authorities and you throw water on it?"

He changed the subject, "You have a good talk with him?" He felt MJ's wide eyes on him.

"Yes, I did. We talked about our lives. The cartel murdered his father and wife. I mentioned how we were running away from a madman..."

Alex held up his hand for silence. "'Sokay, MJ. I don't need to hear. When do we leave? Let's start packing!" He didn't want to hear anymore about this guy.

****

The next morning, Alex and MJ were ready to leave at daybreak. The *federales* were gathered in the inner courtyard as well, along with a number of other motel guests. All headed in the same direction: Mérida.

Roberto explained to those gathered that his group was instructed to follow a marked detour. "The route will take us on a rougher road, up and over the hills, away from the flooding. But the road will be tough. The terrain will be rough. There is no telling where, when, or if, we might run into trouble along the way but we will keep our eyes open."

He finished by saying, "you are all welcome to travel alongside us."

Alex knew this meant he and MJ. A number of other motorists decided they would rather be in the company of the *federales;* they felt safer.

Not surprisingly, an 'incident' happened more than halfway to Mérida. In the afternoon. That's when MJ desperately had to use a washroom. Anything would do. Behind a shrub. A tree. A shack. Anything. But she had to 'go'. And soon.

Alex reluctantly stopped the car and moved out of the 'caravan' so the others could continue. He watched as Roberto's jeep at the head immediately turned around, heading back in their direction. He was obviously keeping an eye on their car.

MJ had already disappeared into the bush.

"Where is she?" he asked, as Alex rolled down his window.

"She had to go to the bathroom," said Alex. "I had to stop. She ran into the bush. Over there."

Roberto jumped from the jeep. He began to scour the roadside bushes.

Suddenly everyone heard it. A scream. High-pitched and terrified.

Instant high alert. The caravan, moving slowly, came to a halt. Car doors opened. People jumped out. The *federales* ordered them back into their cars. No-one knew what was happening. Panic set in. All fears concentrated on a cartel attack.

Suddenly, MJ came tearing back out on the road. Shaking.

Immediately she was surrounded by protective officers. Roberto grabbed her arm. "What happened! What is it?"

Seeing the mobilization reaction and what she had inadvertently caused, MJ broke into tears: "I am sooo sorry."

She cried out to everyone, "Snake! Huge! Long!" She spread wide her arms. "Ready to strike. Right beside me…." She buried her embarrassment in shaking hands.

Roberto wiped his forehead. "Is that all….?" Throwing her a kiss of relief, he ran to his jeep, gave a thumbs up to all those who had been waiting, wondering, and carried on.

But not before yelling "Next stop, Mérida!"

****

Once inside the car again, Alex murmured to MJ: "what was that all about?"

"Oh, Alex. I feel so stupid. So awful. But I had to stop. I had to pee. I'm amazed no-one else has felt the same way. Even worse, I turned my ankle running away from the snake. I can see it's swollen already…."

"Sorry about your ankle but that's not what I meant, MJ. I meant Roberto. And you. Newfound friendship…or more than that?"

MJ fell silent. Looked out the window at the passing greenery. Occasional palm tree. Finally, she spoke, "I've done nothing wrong, Alex. I've just felt an instant bonding with him. Do you know his story….?"

And she started to tell him.

"Not interested, MJ," he said, his eyes straight ahead on the road. "I would be a fool not to notice you two have a mutual attraction."

There was an awkward silence in the car.

"I feel awful, Alex. I'm fond of you but…"

"FOND of me…?" Alex shot back, not taking his eyes off the road. "How can you suddenly have this carnal attraction to a perfect stranger when all along, I thought we had a mutual attraction to each other…"

"We do!" exclaimed MJ. "It's just that…"

"Yes?" said an icy Alex.

"Oh, I don't know, Alex. I truly don't know. It's like he's opened up another part of me. I find him sexual…not that you aren't," she hastened to add, "but he's like an electric charge and I can't seem to get enough and I'm sorry and I feel terrible but I just can't help it."

Alex said nothing. Stared straight ahead, concentrating on his driving.

"You haven't asked about whether or not we've heard from Steve," he said, as if he was dismissing their Roberto conversation.

"Oh, yes. Steve. How could I forget? Have you been in touch, Alex?"

"He called yesterday when you were out romanticizing with Roberto."

MJ winced at his cutting remark. Waited for Alex to continue.

"If he calls me anymore it will be strictly business," said Alex.

"What does that mean?"

"Steve reported that Tommy has left town, apparently the word is he's flying to Mexico."

While moaning and massaging her ankle, MJ felt her stomach lurch.

An old familiar fear erupted inside her. Tommy was coming to claim her, she knew.

Despite the heat, she shivered.

"So now we'll see just how good your Roberto is. Who cares about the cartel when Tommy is on the prowl, looking for us."

Chapter Twenty-Seven

When Rosalie knocked on the front door of the eco-retreat, she casually held her uncle's hand as a show of support. He shoved it away.

"Stop treating me like a convict," he seethed under his breath.

But you are! Rosalie cursed in her mind. *And this might be the only chance you have of redeeming yourself!*

Aloud she said to Martin Garcia, "this is a chance for you to help others and yourself. Mike and Selene are both young and eager to establish a tourist business here. And they've asked to see you. Plus," she added, "they do know your past so you don't have to go over that nightmare again."

The door opened with Selene standing there, in front of Mike, her hand extended in welcome.

"Rosalie, come in," beckoned Mike. "And you must be Martin Garcia. How do you want us to address you: Martin or Garcia? In the tourism business, it helps to keep things simple."

The defrocked priest spoke clearly. And proudly. "Martin is fine. Thank you for seeing me."

It was a strange meeting of confused souls. Mike, dominant and sexually attractive, obviously interested in Rosalie but equally attracted to Selene; Selene, studying this well-educated and good-looking defrocked priest/convicted felon from Brighton, Ontario; Rosalie, also interested in both Mike and Selene; and finally, Martin, the ex-priest, ready to atone for his sins but also arrogant enough to realize he had much to offer, despite his past.

When Mike explained his idea to Martin regarding being an on-site professional therapist for tourists/guests with emotional issues, Martin nodded gravely. This was something he could easily do, having been on the receiving end of countless confessions of the soul.

"The pay isn't so hot," confessed Mike. "at least at first. It all depends on how this idea flies and whether guests in an eco-retreat will respond. We honestly can't afford to pay you anything right now. But if this idea gels and word spreads and more guests come because of your therapy skills, then we can certainly discuss a fair deal."

During the time he was talking, Mike couldn't get over the idea this guy looked familiar. "You always preached in Brighton?" he asked, trying to put a finger on why he felt like he did.

Martin turned to address Rosalie then. In that moment, Mike stared at the man's facial profile. He frowned. Reminded him of….? The nose? No. But something familiar hit him…Martin's eyes? Mannerisms? What the hell was it? He didn't want to pump him about Brighton right now. On this first meeting. Mike did feel comfortable enough with him. As if he'd known/seen him before…He decided he needed time to think over his reaction.

Meanwhile, Selene was facing some interesting introspective questions herself. What was it about this man that seemed familiar? The way he stood and positioned his arms: crossed in front of him…Or was it his voice? She had a strange feeling of *déjà vu* but shook it off. One thing she did notice. The former priest was left-handed. Just as she was. But so what?

Suddenly, from behind them all, Carlos popped into the scene through the open door.

Mike couldn't help himself. "Ah, the clown appears…" he grinned wickedly.

Immediately, Carlos glared in his direction. At the same time, he felt his uncle drinking in the animosity between both men. He knew Martin Garcia would silently file away this mutual dislike in the back of his mind. So, what did Carlos care as long as his uncle was out of his mother's hair and became someone else's problem? Scumbag! How dare he deface their family name, he thought. And in a foreign country! He could only imagine how traumatic it must have been for all those women to testify against a priest. Carlos snorted to himself. Let Mike play his big hero role. He hoped his uncle was so successful that Mike would be up to his ears in reservations and the work that brought. What he wanted was to get his uncle away from his family and home; and get Selene into his world and away from Mike's dominating influence.

At first glance, Carlos didn't see it. But as he chatted with everyone, he became fixated on some of his uncle's mannerisms he never noticed before: the way he stood, arms crossed. Nothing wrong with that but his stance definitely reminded him of someone else, probably his own father. But when he turned to say something to Selene, he suddenly realized she stood the same way. Arms crossed. Same height. Even the shape of his face was similar to Selene's. *Really?* He had never noticed that before. What a strange coincidence.

Suddenly, without warning, Selene, feeling very uncomfortable for some reason, announced:

"Thanks for stopping by, Martin Garcia. I'll leave you with Mike now to fill you in on any details. Right now, Carlos is taking me to the English library in Mérida where I volunteer."

Mike's face looked pinched and puzzled. Carlos was secretly thrilled. Rosalie said simply: "thanks for being here, Selene. And thanks for all your help with this."

Mike's face looked even more pinched as Selene and Carlos rapidly left the eco-retreat office.

****

The next morning, after the chance meeting with Bonnie, and sitting around the *Casa del Balam* pool, Tommy turned to Copley.

"Sounds like we need a visit to this English Library, Cop. Let's make it this afternoon. Not sure where MJ and her runaway boyfriend are right now but obviously this place is where she's meant to work. Can you believe our luck?! Actually, makes me shiver with delight! The gods are shining on me.

Of all the places in all of Mexico we turn up in the right city and stumble, practically fall, into the lap of the lady who's expecting MJ. Like wow! I get an erection just thinking about it…and all the possibilities!"

Copley turned his head away in disgust from his cousin. *Wonder how the chip truck business in Brighton is going? Wonder how Dave is? Haven't checked in with him for awhile. Although no news probably means good news… getting rid of Tommy for awhile is tough. Even though we're in separate rooms. When Tommy is with you, he sticks to you like a leech. Gawd! How did MJ survive all these years? In my heart of hearts, I'm rooting for her to win her freedom battle.*

After their lunch of shrimp tacos, Copley, like a good boy, used his Spanish skills with a desk clerk asking how to get to the English Library that he knew was only a few blocks away.

After a 7 block walk -- when they sauntered into the colonial building-turned-library -- Copley was struck with the immense collection of English language books. Tommy cased the joint for "Bonnie" but saw only lots of other gringos, either volunteers or users. He was impressed with the size and 'busyness' of the place.

Using his fake *really interested* facade, he struck up a conversation with the front desk volunteer. He noticed she was a frump. Why are all librarians he met so dowdy, he wondered? She must have been 50 if she was a day, with greying hair, a dark mole on the right side of her cheek, and under-eye bags so dark she could pass for a raccoon.

"Howdy!" he said brightly.

"Why, hello there," smiled the friendly dowdy frump. "Can I help you?"

"Maybe," he said. "I'm looking for Bonnie."

"Ah, this is her day off. She deserves it….she practically lives here. Something I can help you with?"

"Uh, yes. I – I mean, we, my buddy and me --- happened to meet her yesterday and she mentioned something about a Maya exhibit…..?"

Miss Frump nodded enthusiastically. "Yes. Oh, yes! We are all so excited about this idea. And Bonnie has worked hard to get funding for this new venture. It's to become a permanent part of this library. A place where expats can learn all about the heritage of this area."

And she ran off a practised spiel: "The exhibit will outline the history of the Maya in this area, but more importantly, our aim is to establish a permanent exhibit in English, become *the* centre for Maya history in this state: introduce Maya principles, study their amazing astronomy methods, health practices like their sweat houses (*temazcals,* she proudly explained)*,* medicinal herbs, everything…!"

Tommy could barely stifle a yawn.

"Wow! Exciting! She hiring extra help to get it going?"

"Why, yes. I believe she is. In fact, she expects a couple of volunteers any day now."

"You know them? Not that it's any of our business. But maybe we could add some physical help?" His smile was loaded with charm.

"Well, aren't you thoughtful," said Miss Frump. "One is a young woman from Progreso on the coast and another is from Canada with a special interest in the subject…Not sure if they need any strong men help right now…" And she cast her eyes questioningly on the slightly-built Copley, standing quietly behind Tommy. "You, too?" she queried.

"Oh no. No. No." protested a friendly Tommy on behalf of Copley. "We are both students of the Maya civilization and when she mentioned the project, we thought we'd drop by to learn more. Thank you for your information. You've been more than helpful."

Exit Tommy and Copley from the English Library.

Tommy's grin was almost as wide as a large burrito.

****

Just before entering the Mérida *periférico* (ring road), MJ moaned to Alex…"my ankle is killing me. I'm going to have to get some medical help somewhere here. I can't believe this."

"You want I should ask lover boy for some help or information?" said Alex coldly.

165

After he spoke the words, he watched in the rear-view mirror as Roberto rode up in his jeep behind their car, motioning for them to pull over. Alex watched Roberto exit the black *federale* vehicle and swagger towards them. Jealousy began to erupt and cloud his thinking.

"Alex, MJ," Roberto leaned into the driver's open window. "We are finally here. Obviously." He grinned, pointed to the road sign. Winked at MJ, who returned it with a warm smile.

"I suggest you follow us *federales* while the rest of the folks go their own ways. You two probably need a safe hotel; there is one we stay at each time we are in Mérida. We billet there until our next orders from headquarters. It's in *centro*, a grand example of a fine old hotel. *Casa del Balam* is a favourite among the Spanish gentry. You will find everything you need there: a bar, swimming pool, two *restaurantes* with excellent food, good-sized rooms…." While he was talking, Roberto looked directly at MJ; he barely acknowledged Alex.

MJ was thrilled with his attention. She almost forgot about her Tommy-trauma and panic, and also nearly forgot Alex, who had risked so much to get her this far.

Alex showed no outward reaction but inside he was seething.

Chapter Twenty-Eight

Casa del Balam, *known as the 'grandma' of all hotels in Mérida, is one of the oldest and most distinguished in this capital city of the Yucatán Peninsula. The original owner converted his home to a hotel, keeping its beautiful façade and selecting the name of "Casa del Balam" (Maya words for 'house of the jaguar'). Carrara marble floors, Moorish arches and a stone carved fountain surround its beautiful central courtyard that features tall palms and exotic tropical plants, making it a very special place to mingle. Its clientele includes well-known politicians, performers....*

When MJ hobbled into the *Casa del Balam* with Alex, all she wanted was a shower and a bed. Fully appreciative of the hotel's grandeur, she watched as Alex explored the perimeter of the courtyard with different marble floor passages that led to the exterior pool, bar, and adjoining restaurants.

Squeezed into the small elevator, she and Alex rode to the 5th floor, then stopped to admire the open-to-the-sky courtyard from the waist-high wrought-iron railing. Before collapsing into their room, Alex murmured, *I'd hate to fall over this railing and land on that marble floor.*

MJ smiled weakly. She felt exhausted, mentally and physically. Unsettled stomach. Stabbing headache. Swollen ankle. Raw emotions.

Frantic fear. Somehow, somewhere, she knew Tommy was waiting. She knew she was doomed. It was only a matter of time.

And yet, through all this uncertainty and terror, she felt an overriding, almost irrational, belief that somewhere, somehow, and soon, she would find her daughter here. Her baby hole would heal. And if she found Maya, she was prepared to accept whatever happened later.

Once in their well-appointed room, Alex noted the twin beds with chagrin. He never mentioned this minor observation to MJ whom, he knew, was absolutely wasted and worn down. Intimacy just wasn't in her dictionary right now.

All she wanted, she insisted, was a place to lie down and sleep forever.

As she sat by the window overlooking the *centro* street, she removed her shoes and began massaging her ankle again.

Alex spoke softly to her. "Why don't I go out to explore a bit and if I find a *farmacia,* I'll see what I can get for that sprain. You just lie down."

She nodded, sighed, thanked him, and sank into the comfortable chair. Alex quickly left the room to give her peace.

He had not been gone long when MJ heard a soft tap on her door. Almost as if whoever knocked didn't want to.

"Who is it?" she called.

"Roberto. Just passed Alex in the courtyard on his way out. Everything ok?"

She quickly hobbled to the door, unlocked it, stared at him in disbelief, then grabbed and pulled him in before shutting it. She collapsed into his chest. Sobbing.

"Roberto! Oh, help me please! I'm such a mess and I am so afraid!"

Holding her gently, he quietly led her to the nearest bed.

"Lie down," he said, her hand pressed to his chest. "We need to talk."

And so, MJ poured out her heart again: the search for her daughter; her fear of Tommy; her warm feelings for Alex; her passion for Roberto although they had just met…oh where to go? What to do?

In reply, Roberto leaned over to comfort with a light touch to her cheek. Instantly, she grabbed him, her fatigue suddenly vanished; pulled him down beside her, smothering him with soft kisses. She inhaled his masculinity. Felt his hardness. Her pulse pounded. That breathless catch in the pit of her stomach seized, overwhelmed her.

At once he enveloped her in warm, strong arms, holding her fast then tormenting her with gentle nibbles and urgent nips. Forehead, eyes, nose, nape of her neck, earlobes, and finally her eagerly open mouth. He probed in and around with his tongue.

MJ was on fire. Cried out like a kitten. Pulled him down.

His searching mouth roved over her waiting body, stopping long enough to send her into spasms of pleasure.

After tearing off her white top, she ripped open his black shirt.

Drowning in desire, he tasted her moistness: tongue to tongue, tongue to body, tongue in her most sacred places. Maddeningly slowly, tenderly, he continued to undress her, pausing to drink in her quivering body.

They both heard the card click in the door at the same time.

****

From outside his 7th floor hotel room, standing at the wrought-iron safety railing, casually watching the comings and goings of the hotel lobby, Tommy suddenly, silently, lit up with OMG! Were his eyes deceiving him? Had he actually seen MJ cross the courtyard floor with that stupid clod saviour of hers, heading for the elevator!?

Like, how lucky was he?! This totally delightful happenstance almost had him dancing and clicking his heels. Plus -- he chuckled with an inner glee – he knew exactly where she would be when she wasn't in the hotel: the English library! Oh, don't ever doubt there is a god somewhere, he hummed. He as good as had her back right now! Wonder what floor she's on? What's her room number? Where *is* that stupid Copley? He can find out everything at the front desk.

****

MJ felt awful. Physically ill. As much as she adored Roberto, the last thing in the world she wanted to do was hurt Alex.

But hurt him she did. When he walked in on her and Roberto in the hotel room, MJ felt like a cheap tramp. No amount of explanation would help Alex understand her feelings. With him, she felt warm and wonderful. But not vibrant, exciting, and sexual. Like she felt with Roberto.

After Roberto left the room, quickly, fully dressed, but not apologetic, Alex was forced to face the truth. While his relationship with MJ was deep, hers with him was superficial. He hid his hurt, blinking back tears. After a short, civil discussion, they both agreed the best thing was for him to take a separate room.

No, she insisted. *I will be the one to move. I have violated your trust in me.* And she did. To a room on the 7th floor. The same floor as Roberto, where the *federales* were usually quartered.

Alone in her new room, thankful to Alex for the elastic bandage he bought on his *centro* walk-around, she snugly wrapped her ankle, called for a taxi at the desk, and was driven the few blocks to the English library.

171

Chapter Twenty-Nine

Before Carlos dropped Selene off at the English Library in Mérida, he leaned over to caress her cheek. Selene smiled. "I'm glad we had this time alone to talk with each other, Carlos. You can tell I'm a bit mixed up right now. But I'll get myself sorted out soon." She added softly, "With you."

Carlos nodded imperceptibly. Watched her beautiful figure disappear into the library.

Inside, Selene saw Bonnie immediately who smiled. "Hey, lady! Great to see you! Guess what? We've heard from MJ, the woman from Canada I was telling you about. She's arrived in Mérida and we're expecting her this afternoon. Now we can get on with our Maya project!"

****

When MJ walked into the English Library, she did not expect to see such a lively and active facility. Also, a surprisingly large one. Her thoughts had focused on a smaller building but this one surpassed her expectations. The front -- an old Spanish colonial home façade – gave way to a grand interior, complete with the usual bookshelves but, at the back, an open-to-the-sky balcony was alive with greenery: royal palms, oleander flowering shrubs, the sacred ceiba tree of the Maya, bougainvillea…

MJ stood stunned, admiring this beautiful setting. How her library friend Glenda, back home, would drool over this! No wonder she wanted to link this library with the Brighton one and bring the Maya world to life. Glenda had a wonderful vision and MJ was thrilled to be part of it.

But first things first, she mused. She was nervous about finally meeting this young woman, Selene Rupert, whose news article about opening an eco-resort first drove MJ to thinking about coming here. She recalled her excitement: how could she ever have thought Selene could be her long-lost daughter? She was really grasping at straws.

Now, standing here alone in this wonderful library, looking around at the books, and volunteers, and members, she knew how wrong she'd been. What had driven her to such a conclusion? But inside she knew: a mother's hope. Trying to close that baby hole she carried in her heart.

"Hi there. Can I help you?"

Lost in reverie, MJ spun around, quickly apologizing to a pleasant older woman whom she assumed was a volunteer.

"Oh yes, please. I'm looking for Bonnie."

Immediately she was directed to a small office behind the Main Entry desk. "You'll find her in there. At least I think so. You may have to move a few books to find her."

MJ cautiously knocked and slowly opened the door. "Bonnie?" she half-whispered.

From behind a mountain of books, a pleasant woman's face appeared. "Hi. Can I help?"

“Hi. I’m MJ….”

“From Canada!” Bonnie almost screeched. “Welcome! Hurray! Selene is coming in this afternoon. I’ll text her. Finally, we meet! How was your car trip here? Heard you got held up because of flooding! You’ve had quite the experience. Welcome! Welcome!” Bonnie exclaimed as she came around her desk, embracing MJ with a hug.

“We are all so excited! I’ll email Glenda to let her know you’ve finally arrived. Coffee? Let me bring you up to date with where we’re at and our exciting plans!”

MJ inhaled Bonnie’s energy. She nodded for coffee. Breathing deeply, she felt she was ‘home’.

****

“And so finally we meet,” said MJ, extending her hand in greeting to Selene. She couldn’t get over how sweaty her palms had become. For some reason, she avoided the younger woman’s eyes, as if looking at them would betray any alternate intentions.

“Yes, finally,” agreed Bonnie. “Selene is an amazing young woman, a real go-getter.”

Selene shook MJ’s hand. Lightly. Carefully. She did not pump it. She paused before speaking. Finally, “this should be an exciting project. How is it you’re so interested in the Maya?”

Her question threw MJ off-balance. “Not sure,” she smiled. “I can’t believe how lucky I am to be here and work with you both on this project.”

175

"Let's get started, shall we?" said Bonnie. "I'll take you over the physical aspects of our project, then our approach, and finally, how best to arrange it. We hope to integrate some of the exhibit around the Maya sacred tree, the ceiba, that we have growing around our balcony."

While MJ and Selene listened carefully, Bonnie expanded on her plans. During her presentation, MJ stole glances at Selene, trying to study her without being noticed. Selene's facial features, her nose in particular, seemed similar to MJ. Or was it her imagination? Selene was left-handed; MJ was not. Still, the younger woman's stance, mannerisms, definitely reminded her of herself. Her eyes? And the way she spoke…was there a similarity or only her imagination?

Then, just as she talked herself out of the thought, Bonnie interjected unexpectedly. "My goodness," she heard Bonnie say "If I didn't know better, I'd swear you two were sisters!"

Both women laughed. A similar laugh. It was true, though, they seemed to have some innate bonding. Following a two-and-a-half-hour intense session, Bonnie held up her hand. "Let's quit for now. I don't want to scare either of you with any more details. Besides, I have another meeting in half an hour! I'm leaving you two alone now."

MJ and Selene smiled at each other. Selene was the first to speak.

"Since you're new here, how'd you like to come to our eco-retreat for a swim? Maybe tomorrow?" she suggested. "You need to get out of this city. It can get stifling hot!"

MJ pointed to her elastic-wrapped ankle. "Sounds great," she replied. "And it may even do my ankle some good." Why did she think she was talking to her long-lost daughter? This exotic-looking beauty before her, with the pierced jewel on the side of her nose…it didn't seem plausible or possible. Although their voices were similar and once, when Selene laughed, MJ did a double-take. She noticed an MJ similarity in the lilt of her laugh.

"My boyfriend's picking me up now," said Selene. "Want a drive?"

MJ shook her head. "Thanks, but no. I want to spend some time in this library before we get so involved in our project, I won't have time. But I will take you up on your offer to go for a swim at your eco-retreat tomorrow. If that's okay…"

"Of course," smiled Selene with a smile that looked familiar to MJ. "See you tomorrow then…"

After her departure, before heading back to the hotel, MJ wandered through the library, thinking about Bonnie's innocent 'sister' comment. She turned to saunter along one of the shelves. From the corner of her eye, she glimpsed a familiar figure. Stopped. Stared. *Is that who I think it is?* she frowned. *It couldn't be…*Copley?!

Then her heart stopped. She almost gagged. Stifled a scream. Right behind Copley – grinning -- leering at her – loomed Tommy.

MJ couldn't get out of there fast enough. Without a backward glance, she had the desk volunteer call a taxi, jumped into it, and didn't feel safe until she reached *Casa del Balam*. Completely disoriented, she grabbed her room key and hid inside her room.

OhmyGod! She repeated over and over again. Tommy! He had found her! What in God's name was she going to do? Tell Alex? No. Hardly fair. Tell Roberto? At least he knew about Tommy. Plus, he was armed. Those *federales* know how to handle violence and MJ knew how violent Tommy was. Then she should warn Alex! It was only fair. He tried to attack him before…back home! Oh, what to do? What to do? Internally, she was a mess.

Somehow, MJ survived that night. She called room service for food, double-bolted her door, and lay quivering, despite the heat, in bed all night with the TV on. Her scattered mind tried to make plans. And when should she alert Alex? And Roberto, whom she knew was on duty manoeuvres throughout the city?

Thankfully, she heard from both Alex and Roberto via her cell that evening. Alex wanting to know how her time went at the library and how was she? Roberto asking almost the same things but also expressing how he longed to be with her. Feel her. Have her feel him…She almost dissolved into phone sex.

By dawn, she decided she was going to act as normally as possible. She was going to return to the library via taxi, work on the Maya project with Bonnie and Selene, and then take up Selene's offer to swim in her eco pool in Progreso. This way she could keep her eyes open for Tommy. Plus, she'd be out of the city for awhile.

Obviously, she decided, Tommy had tracked her to the library, which, when she thought about it did make sense with her yapping about that article right in front of him.

At least she felt safe here in the hotel with both Roberto and Alex nearby. But how in God's name – and when – did Tommy arrive? And why was Copley with him? Questions. Questions, that drove her crazy while her mind whirled like a fan.

***

The following day -- in the eco-retreat outside of Progreso -- Big Mike was showing Rosalie and Martin Garcia (Mike was calling him *MG* now) the retreat's features: naturally turquoise-coloured swimming pool fed by clean underground water, the environmentally responsible rooms with their dehydrating compostable toilets and water-from-rainfall shower stalls, large gardens of organic vegetables, and their sustainable hives for the beneficial Maya melipona bees. "The species are trying to make a comeback," said Mike. "We're doing our part to help them."

Rosalie seemed impressed. MG looked bored.

Mike had decided beforehand that he'd better get MG on board with all aspects of the retreat if the ex-priest was going to 'work' here; naturally he invited Rosalie as well. He was getting used to having her around. And liked it.

MG was impressed, too, except he was damned he'd show it. As a priest, he was used to others looking up to him, kowtowing to him. Ever since he'd been deported and forced to return home, he'd been struggling with trying to maintain a balance between humble ex-priest and the haughty sexual predator he knew he still was. He couldn't help himself. Even the psychiatrist he'd been forced to see told him he was addicted to sex. Should never have entered the holy sanctity of priesthood. MG admitted he yearned for the feel of a moist vulva, especially a young one. He thought he'd better keep away from Rosalie, play the pious priest with her since she was a relative. But that Selene girl raised more than his interest. *Maybe playing a social counsellor for this Mike Prick might work out after all,* he reasoned. *But right now, back to reality. What was the Prick was saying? Seems he stopped his diatribe. Taking a call on his cell from Selene.*

"Carlos and Selene are on their way here with a guest, it seems," said Mike. "Someone called MJ, works with Selene at the library. Selene thought she'd like a swim in our eco pool. You're both welcome to stay," he said, looking only at Rosalie.

She nodded. "That would be great! I hate to admit it but I'm actually wearing my bathing suit under this dress, hoping to get the chance."

Mike turned to MG. "And you?"

"Of course, thank you, Mike," replied the former priest. It pained him to feel so ingratiated towards this holier-than-thou guy.

****

When Selene, Carlos, and MJ arrived at the eco-retreat, Selene whisked MJ away to her private room so they could change into their bathing suits. MJ was delighted when she saw the turquoise sisal carpet of the Maya Corn God. Just being here, with Selene, calmed her jumpy nerves.

And that's when 'it' happened.

Selene had turned her back to slip on her bikini. MJ inadvertently took a casual glance at Selene's perfect skin and then gasped. Aloud. She saw the birthmark. Small. Round. Flat. Dark brown. *At the bottom of her baby's spine*. The Maya circle: *wa* – and 24 years melted away.

Selene whirled around. "Aha," she said, "I bet you're wondering about that tat at the bottom of my back, *Man N'enex* -- the Maya word for *welcome*. That was done years ago when I used to drink a lot. I've grown to like it."

MJ just stared. *At her daughter.* In a whirlwind moment, suddenly everything made sense. It was all coming together. She had stumbled on Maya, her birth daughter. No wonder Bonnie thought they looked like sisters. No wonder she'd felt such an affinity with this warm, welcoming, beautiful young woman who was also smitten with the Maya. But MJ said nothing. Fear of rejection? Not the right time or place? Instead, she took a deep breath and said, "you are obviously like me…attracted to the Maya".

If MJ was not prepared to identify Selene as her daughter right now, she was totally unprepared for her next discovery. It hit her like a double whammy.

****

As both women emerged from Selene's private room, they joined the others around the eco-pool. Except for Carlos whom MJ now knew, Selene casually introduced the others to MJ, who smiled, shook hands, despite her still-quivering insides.

"MJ, this is Rosalie, cousin of Carlos; and Mike, my business partner. And this," she turned to the former priest, "is Martin Garcia, our retreat's counsellor to lost souls…."

MJ gulped. Pushed down the bile rising in her throat. Stared at the face of the priest she would never, ever forget no matter his age. Her former tormentor. Her rapist. Her baby's father…

"Sorry," she hastily apologized, withdrawing her hand. "I'm suddenly not feeling very well." Gagging, she turned to Carlos, "do you mind taking me back to the hotel? Please? I know it's a huge request but I think I'm coming down with something and I don't want to spread it to anyone."

Chapter Thirty

Back at the *Casa del Balam,* MJ raced to Alex's room, pounding on the door. No answer. She called his cell. "Where are you?" she gasped.

"Sitting around the pool. Outside," he said casually. "What's up?"

"I need to talk to you, Alex. Now! Please!"

"kay. Come on down why don't you? Very pleasant here in the sun with a drink in my hand. Want me to order a marguerita for you?"

"Be there in a minute…just wait there."

OMG, she thought when she saw Alex sitting there. *He is such a sweetheart. What is the matter with me? I have hurt him so badly and he has been so good to me. But, I can't help my feelings for Roberto. He is so exciting.* And then, she suddenly realized, *I never gave Alex a chance.*

"Alex," she said breathlessly, drawing up a poolside chair beside him. "Tommy is here."

The effect on Alex was dramatic. "What? Where? Did you see him? Worse, did he see you?!"

Sitting safely beside him, she poured out everything. She even spilled out that she was certain Selene was her daughter. And that her rapist, that awful, hideous priest, was at this eco-lodge.

Alex could scarcely digest her news. "Are you sure, MJ? About Selene? About the priest? About Tommy? Are you absolutely sure?!"

"Why would I make this up? I'm a mess. I don't know who to turn to, what to do."

"So, you came to me." He said flatly.

MJ bowed her head. "I'm so sorry, Alex...."

"What about lover boy...hot stuff Roberto? Maybe he could help....?"

MJ looked away. "I'm so sorry, Alex, so sorry," she whispered. "I just came to let you know about Tommy because he tried to kill you once...."

"Because I was trying to free his hostage. Remember that, MJ?"

She hung her head.

Alex sighed. "It's okay, MJ. Well, not okay. But you've been honest with me and that counts."

She smiled crookedly at him. He returned the smile. Leaned towards her so their foreheads touched. "You know I've always loved you, MJ."

"Oh, please, Alex...please, please don't add to my misery. I love you, too, but...."

"...You love me like a brother?" he countered. Then he smiled his sweet, crooked smile. "MJ, I'll do anything for you. You know that, don't you? And right now, much as I hate to say this, you need Roberto. He can protect you better than me."

"I won't be seeing him until he gets back from manoeuvres tonight."

"Tell him then. I'll be with you, if you like, to fill in the blanks."

Chapter Thirty-One

Tommy was grinning. Sipping his *Patron* tequila in the hotel bar, he turned to Copley.

"Well, isn't this a humdinger of a situation," he said with an evil smirk. "Here we are in the same hotel as MJ and that Alex creep and they don't even know it yet. I'm telling you, Cop, I can barely stand this suspense! When I look at my options, they are all winners: I grab MJ and we force her back with us on the plane. I fight off that Alex creep and maybe kill him with some sucker punches… and to make certain he's dead, I have my hunting knife. Great for skinning animals and cutting up nasty enemies."

Copley gulped. "C'mon Tommy. Let's not get into violence. We're in a foreign country and …"

"…and what, Cop? This is México, for God's sake, where murders happen all the time and no-one takes any notice. Why, we've almost got an open license-to-kill!" He was almost beside himself with excitement.

"Here's my plan, Cop." He lowered his voice. "Those two lily-white idiots don't even know we're all staying in the same hotel. My plan is for you to find out what room MJ is in and let me know. I'll handle the rest."

****

185

Later that evening, as MJ waited in her hotel room for Roberto to return, she thought about her discussion with Alex. *He is such a sweetheart,* she sighed. *Such a sweetheart...*

Knock. Knock.. *Roberto!* She hurried, despite her bad ankle, to answer. Pulled back the chain…

"Gotcha!" Tommy lunged at her with his knife to her throat, stuffing a facecloth in her mouth. Grabbed her arms behind her back, kneed her from there, dragged her to his room down the hall. She tried to scream but couldn't.

Tommy loved the terror in her eyes. Like a wild animal knowing it was hopeless to fight.

"I told you, MJ, I'd get you and take you back and I meant every damn word of it!" he hissed into her ear. "We've got some talking to do! And you better listen to everything I say!"

"But first," he breathed in triumph, "I'm going to tie you to that bed and fuck you like you've never been fucked before, you little tramp! Maybe use the knife, too. And no use screaming, *milady,* cuz the gag stays put!"

****

When Roberto returned to the hotel later that evening and tried to reach MJ, he was puzzled. She didn't answer her cell, or the knock on her room door. He hated to do it, but he contacted Alex.

Alex was immediately on high alert. He repeated everything he knew to Roberto but was at a loss to know where MJ could have gone. He was positive she would never leave the hotel. Indeed, he was sure she would have told him, now knowing Tommy was on the loose. Her last words were that she intended to tell Roberto everything, trusting Alex would add his comments.

Roberto suggested they convince the hotel staff to open MJ's door. As a *federale,* Roberto knew no questions would be asked.

When the staff member knocked on MJ's hotel door on the 7th floor, and there was no reply, he used his card to release the lock. Roberto and Alex rushed in. Quickly, they saw signs of a scuffle: an overturned table lamp, a spilled glass of water….and then, together, they all heard a scream.

Rushing out the door, they figured the scream came from the same floor only a few doors away. Suddenly, the door to a room was thrown open.

With horror, they saw MJ -- pushed from behind -- landing hard on the concrete floor, hands tied behind her back. After her flew out Tommy, armed with a knife, followed by a frightened Copley.

The next few minutes blurred: Tommy lunged with his knife at a shocked and unprepared Alex; as blood spurted from his chest, Alex collapsed on the floor.

And then, suddenly, Copley hurled himself from behind making a direct hit on Tommy – knocking him off-balance – so Copley could easily push him over the railing. He would never forget Tommy's howl as he fell to the marble courtyard below.

Roberto ran to MJ's side.

***

"It was Copley who saved me," claimed a weeping MJ after the horrible events on the 7th floor were 'cleaned up'/handled by Roberto, the hotel staff, and municipal police forces. "He was the one who came into Tommy's room and told him to stop. Stop attacking me. Stop hating everyone. Stop what he was doing…" She paused. "If it hadn't been for Copley, I wouldn't be here." She stopped. Sobbed. "But maybe Alex would. Oh Alex! I am so sorry….!" And she dropped her head in her hands and wept again.

"I hated that man," said Copley, sitting beside Roberto on a wooden chair in a room on the hotel's ground floor, telling his side of the story to municipal detectives. In fluent Spanish, he continued: "he bullied me when I was a kid. Pretended he had my best interests at heart whenever he fought someone 'on my behalf'. But all he wanted was to let everyone know he was Big Bad Tommy and if you didn't agree with him, he'd pulverize you."

Copley continued: "He captured MJ when she was at her most vulnerable. An unwed mother, thrown out of the house by her real mother, nowhere to go - her father had already left – she was penniless, lost the only human being she loved, her daughter, who had been placed for a quick adoption – and onto this scene comes Big-Hearted Tommy. Ha! What a crock!

"I knew what he was doing. Kept her a prisoner all those years -- ask her if she was his sex slave – I think she was. She had no choice. She was 16 and as naïve as a puppy when he 'saved' her. Ask her!

"Then I read about this weird mental illness when a captive begins to admire and fall in love with the captor. I honestly believe that's what happened with MJ. And when she began to think for herself…and realize there was a big world out there she could enjoy, she naturally wanted out. But no," he continued, "he didn't want a thinking woman. He wanted someone he could bully and control. Time and time again, I saw it. But I didn't have the guts to do anything about it. Because I was weak, stupid, gay, skinny Copley who couldn't fend for himself and needed Big Bad Tommy as his protector. Bullshit!

"When I met Dave and we travelled the world and decided to live together in a small town like Brighton, we knew we were taking our chances. But the world is changing, more accepting of people like me. But Tommy?" he paused. "He could never accept living with a man. And he could never accept losing MJ. No-one trusted him. No-one would care if he died or dried up and floated away. That was the one thing Tommy couldn't understand…that no-one liked him. Everyone hated him! He got away with what he did because it was well-known he would retaliate in the most brutal way."

Notes were taken while a tape recorder whirred.

"And so, yes. I knowingly and deliberately pushed Tommy to his death over that railing. To save MJ and countless others in the future."

Copley stopped.

Roberto turned to Copley, sitting beside him. Placing a strong hand on his shoulder, he asked him to stand as they embraced each other.

MJ cried again.

****

Later, after a week's hiatus, MJ returned to the English Library to continue with the project she and Selene had started with Bonnie.

When MJ watched Selene walk towards her – the same gait as her own – she decided today was the day she would sit down and explain why she knew Selene was her long-lost daughter, Maya.

Somehow, MJ knew, although Selene would face disbelief and tears and misgivings and rantings and ravings, she and her Maya would find peace as mother and daughter. The baby hole would heal.

And together – she, Maya and Roberto -- would address the sins of Martin Garcia…

About the Author

Heather Rath is the award-winning author of *Stalker*, a collection of critically acclaimed and thought-provoking short stories.

Searching for Maya is Rath's much anticipated first novel - and it too has the literary world taking note of this gifted writer with a knack for blending all too human stories with a thriller's intrigue and hidden dangers.

Ever since she won a city-wide writing contest for elementary students in Ottawa, Canada, Rath knew writing would be a major part of her life. When she grew up, she was sequentially a reporter, editor of a weekly newspaper and a monthly business magazine before becoming head of communications for a multi-national company. During this time, she edited, and contributed to, two anthologies of southwestern Ontario writers.

The award-winning writer has been published widely over the years in various publications and some of her work for children has been translated into Braille.

She is a member of CANSCAIP (Canadian Society of Children's Authors, Illustrators & Performers), Canadian Authors Association and an associate member of Crime Writers of Canada.

Family, writing, and travel are her passions. She invites you to visit her website www.heatherrath.net

Manor House
www.manor-house-publishing.com
905-648-4797